MW00411802

Liar, Liar

Liar, Liar

Gabrielle Williams

KENSINGTON PUBLISHING CORP.
http://www.kensingtonbooks.com

This is a work of fiction. The author stresses that none of the characters in this book are in any way, shape or form representations of the following people: Andrew, Lindy, Kate, Ross, Liz, Sally, Reidy, Tim, Simonette, Andrew, Hendo, Sarah, Sam, Alison, Margie, Peter, Simone, David, Leah, Greg, Anne, Scott, Carol, Kieran, the Sargoods, Tim, Sam, Doug, Pete, Luke, Clare, Adam, Doone, Chris, Gin, Tim, Anna, Phil Annelies, Dave, Kate, Eric, Maria, Danno, Jo, or any of the 100 richest men in Australia.

STRAPLESS BOOKS are published by

Kensington Publishing Corp.
850 Third Avenue
New York, NY 10022

Copyright © 2001 by Gabrielle Williams. First published in Australia in 2001 by HarperCollinsPublishers Pty Limited. This edition published by arrangement with HarpercollinsPublishers Pty Limited. Original title is *Two canadian clubs and dry at the martini den*.

All rights reserved. No part of this book may be reproduced in any form or by any means without the prior written consent of the Publisher, excepting brief quotes used in reviews.

All Kensington titles, imprints, and distributed lines are available at special quantity discounts for bulk purchases for sales promotion, premiums, fund-raising, educational or institutional use.

Special book excerpts or customized printings can also be created to fit specific needs. For details, write or phone the office of the Kensington Special Sales Manager: Kensington Publishing Corp., 850 Third Avenue, New York, NY, 10022. Attn. Special Sales Department. Phone: 1-800-221-2647.

Strapless and the Strapless logo are trademarks of Kensington Publishing Corp. Kensington and the K logo Reg. U.S. Pat. & TM Off.

ISBN 0-7582-0613-5

First Kensington Trade Paperback Printing: December 2003
10 9 8 7 6 5 4 3 2 1

Printed in the United States of America

For Andrew, Dominique, Harry and Charlie.
Oh, and Brutus.

Chapter 1

The Martini Den. Just off Collins Street in the city. So hot, so hip, so happening, so today, it's probably gone off the boil by the time you read this. A Cary Grant/Grace Kelly-type bar in the city. A bit of a hairspray-and-kitten-heels-type place. A Canadian-Club-with-dry-ginger-type hangout. Lots of liquid eyeliner, schmoozing and general glamorousness.

It's practically compulsory to smoke. And when you do smoke, it's really satisfying because the whites of the lights pick up the smoke as you exhale, giving it a thick, fluffy, good-enough-to-eat-type look.

Minnow had never been there until he went there that night.

Elli went there all the time.

Standing in a group, Elli stands out. She's very dark: black hair, dark skin and dark eyes. Dark, dark, dark. She has these big Italian boobs which she always wears up and perky, like her hair. She piles her hair on top of her head, messy, and she piles her boobs on top of her chest, neat.

She wears simple clothes, very expensive, and the only way she can afford them on her waitress wage is by careful selection and multiple wears. Her coat in the cloakroom of The Martini Den that night is black wool, very fitted, very Audrey Hepburn, with an RRP of $750. But so far it's only cost her $3.50. Approximately. That's calculated on a per outing basis. She has worn it every day all winter. That's 200 days. 200 goes into 750 about 3.5 times. $3.50. For a winter coat. Not bad.

But she's not wearing the coat when Minnow first sees her. (It's in the cloakroom, remember.) No, when Minnow first notices her, she's wearing black bootleg pants (Scanlan & Theodore, $379, worn most days this winter, say, 120 days. One hundred and twenty goes into 379 three times with a bit left over, so they're worth about $3 something) with a vibrant red fitted top (Morrisey, $210, worn at least once a week for six months, that's twenty-six weeks. You do the maths).

Some girls can't help but make an impression. Elli is one of them. Boys just love her. Uh-huh, yes they do, no question. She's so voluptuous, so womanly, so exotic, that guys think of sex as soon as they see her. She stands at the bar, but they don't see her standing at the bar. They see her stretched out beneath them, eyes half-closed, mouth half-open, enjoying a good rogering, courtesy of their own good, skillful selves.

So this particular night, Elli was at The Martini Den with a few of the guys from work — Tristan, Chris, Philby, Johnno, Adam and Luke (don't bother remembering their names, you don't need them for later) — and she noticed this cute guy standing with a group at the bar. At least he looked cute considering it was bloody hard to see with the lights down so low. Not one of the usuals. Wasn't with anyone she knew. Just some cute guy out late at night with a bunch of friends. Tall and skinny, just how she liked them. His clothes were kind of casual, kind of loose, and right up to the absolute second, although he had a kind of couldn't-give-a-shit-type look about him. Short hair, a bit messy. On another guy it would have looked like too much effort had been put into it, but this guy looked like he had naturally messy, just-fucked hair. Stubble. Not too much. Like he'd had a shave that morning and there was a bit of late-night growth happening. The overall effect was definitely working for Elli. She continued glancing over to suss out his personality.

Did he look vain (he didn't), did he look like fun (yes), did he have a girlfriend (didn't seem to), was he popular (looked like it), was he drunk (not too pissed), what did his friends look like (groovy) and was there a chance he might be interested in her (disappointingly, no).

He didn't look at her. Not once. If he had've, she would have looked away, because she's not into giving some anonymous guy the full-on eyeball, even if he does look really cute. Because, after all, it's late and dark, and the next morning he might not seem such a catch, so it's best not to go there in the first place. But the least he could have done is looked. At least once. Just a bit of a critical assessment on his part. Feeling up her body with his eyes. That's all.

For godsake, she wasn't an eyesore and she'd done her fair share of once-overing him — he couldn't possibly have not noticed. It started her thinking. There was a time when every guy in the room had her flat on her back before she'd even sat down, and she had hated it. It offended her. It made her feel icky, like they felt she was public property. But now that Mr Handsome over there wasn't even vaguely checking her out, she felt a bit miffed. And to be honest, a little concerned. After all, she was nearly thirty. Maybe she'd lost her touch? That happens, you know. Or maybe her pheromones weren't quite as potent anymore. Maybe she hadn't lost her touch. Maybe she'd lost her scent. It wasn't out of the question. This kind of thing probably happens to the aged, the elderly. Thirty-year-olds.

Like Elli's grandma. What was that odour she exuded? I'm telling you, it ain't pheromones. It smelt a bit dusty or something. A kind of mouldy lavendery stench leaching to the surface, oozing out of her pores.

Ugh. She needed a drink.

'A Canadian Club and dry, thanks,' she said.

'Make that two.'

She looked across, and then up, and there he was, standing a bit too close in a bar that wasn't really that crowded, grinning like some kind of stupid grinning-thingo.

Now she could ignore him. Now that he had shown a degree of interest, she could settle down, relax, and not worry about him. For one thing, up close he looked quite young, 24 or 25. Cute, definitely, but young. Possibly a bit too handsome for his own good. Possibly cocky. Possibly gets every single girl he ever makes a move on, so the challenge for Elli was not to let him get her. Flirt a bit maybe. Probably. But that's all. That's it. Nothing else.

'Hi,' he said.

Cute smile, very cute. A bit too cute, if you'd asked Elli.

'Hi,' she said, smiling back.

Sexy. Lips like plums. Tasty. Ripe. A bit swollen. The sort of mouth that looked like it had no trouble getting around some words — words like 'bed' and 'penis' and 'sex' and 'headjob'. A mouth that he'd really like to see experimenting with those words. Oooh, yeah.

'Whisky's not normally a girl's drink,' he said.

'You don't think so?'

And it went on from there. Inane. The meaning of each word unimportant. Just moving mouths making words,

4

making conversation, making shapes. Watching the shapes each other's mouths made. The shape her eyes made when she looked up at him. The shape his body made when he leaned towards her. Each word an excuse to watch the other and think of shapes they could make together. The missionary shape, for example. The 69 shape.

'So. Did you kiss him?' Daphne asked the next day.
'Yeah.'
'Is he going to call?'
'I don't think so.'
'Why not?'
'I think me saying I had a kid put him off.'
'What?!'

'So. Did you fuck her?' his mates asked. Pronounced 'jevuker'.
'Nahbeda.'
'Nahbeda' doesn't mean anything. It used to. It used to be shorthand for 'nah, but I fingered her' back in Minnow's school days, when getting your hands down a 15-year-old private schoolgirl's knickers had real cachet. Probably still does with some people. But now 'nahbeda' means nothing. It doesn't mean he didn't fuck her, it doesn't mean he did. It's just the 'good, how are you?' to a friend's 'hi, how it's going?' Just the thing you say. Kind of like the boy plug to the girl socket. Just fits together without too much thought going into it.

Minnow and Elli left The Martini Den at about 4:30 a.m., both a little more smashed, both a little more into each other. Not holding hands though. Not yet. And no arms around each other. Just the occasional touch, as if one of them was having trouble hearing what the other was saying and needed to move in a bit closer.

Walking down Collins Street towards Elli's car, a guy slouching past asked them for some money. Minnow gave him a couple of bucks.

'You know, that's not bad,' Elli said.

'What?'

'That guy just made $2, and it took him less than a minute. So if he does that full time, 40 hours a week, he'd make a fortune. He's probably some kind of millionaire.'

'Yeah. Maybe I should do that. I'm looking for worth-while employment.'

'And if you picked your targets, you'd do even better. Like, you could work the legal end of the city and there'd only be lawyers, and they'd probably dish out $5 bills, instead of $2 coins.'

'Or you could target multi-millionaires, and they'd probably dole out $100 bills.'

'Even better.'

Silence. Walking in silence.

'How would you know they were multi-millionaires, though?' Elli asked.

'By all the people trying to scab money off them, I s'pose,' Minnow said.

Elli laughed.

And then, there was her car.

'This is my car.'

Damn.

And so she rummaged through her bag looking for her keys, wondering if they were going to kiss or not. Or if he was going to ask for her phone number. And would she see him again? And what was she thinking? He was at least five years younger than her and even though he was cute, she didn't really want him to ring because he was probably into football and rock climbing and racing motorbikes, and all things that she wasn't into. And besides all that, he wasn't Ben and he never would be. And she couldn't help thinking about Ben even though it wasn't happening with him anymore because he was now with some chick called Kate, and Kate had a kid and they were busy playing happy families. Anyway, what was Ben doing with her? She was a mother, for fuck's sake, and she couldn't possibly be as good a cook as Elli and she couldn't be half as much fun. And then Minnow leaned into her thoughts.

'Bye.'

He put his hand behind her head and kissed her softly on the mouth. It was a gentle, lingering pressing of lips together and he said, 'That's nice.'

Then he leaned forward again and started kissing her, tasting her. He moved his body closer to hers, and he felt really warm and strong. His arms moved to circle her and she leaned into him, and it didn't matter at all that he was probably five years younger than her. It didn't matter that he wasn't Ben, although, come to think of it, it sort of did matter. What was she doing thinking of Ben at a time like this? She stepped backwards and Minnow looked at her, nuzzled forward and asked her back to his place.

'Come back to my place.'

And she really wanted to but she knew she wasn't ready for anything, and she wasn't interested in sleeping with him just for the sake of it. Although, she could feel that same yum feeling spreading through her body that she recognised from all those times with Ben. She knew she had to stop it quick before anything happened, because it just wasn't right. And then she said:

'I can't come back to your place.'

And he murmured, 'Come on. Come back.'

And she said, 'I can't, because I like to be at home when my kid wakes up in the morning.'

And he stepped back from her.

What?

The 'K' word. 'Kid'. Even worse than 'kommitment'.

There he was, on Collins Street, 4:30 on a Wednesday morning, just back from a year overseas, and he's locking lips with a m-o-t-h-e-r. He felt like a dirty old pervert. He couldn't believe it. He'd had her pegged for someone completely different. A mother of all things! Well, one thing was certain. One thing he knew for sure. The one thing he wasn't was a mother-fucker. No way, no how. He was too young for that kind of crap. A kid. I mean, sure, one day maybe. But tomorrow morning? Uh-uh.

'But I don't get it. What made you say you had a kid?'

'I don't know.'

'Didn't you want to see him again? He sounds cute.'

'I'm not sure. I don't know. It was just one of those things. It kind of came out.'

'Besides, she had a kid.'

'No way. You kissed someone's mother?'

'Yeah.'

'Gross.'

'No, she was nice, but you know . . .'

A bit of silence. They were both thinking. It was like that time Doug was in Thailand and that boy/girl tried to kiss him and Doug didn't even realise it was a she-male until the very last second. Thank God the hands had given it away and he hadn't kissed him. Her. It.

Then Doug said: 'You know what that would have made you, if you'd slept with her.'

'Yeah.'

'A mother-fucker.'

'Yeah, I'm on to it.'

Chapter 2

Elli leant back against the kitchen sink, wearing a white singlet and striped pyjama bottoms, arms folded under her boobs. She watched Daphne scratch marmalade onto her toast.

'You know,' said Elli, 'I've done the sex thing. I've done the drugs thing. I drive a car. I have a job. But I don't think I'll really feel like a grown-up until I wake up one morning and choose to have marmalade on my toast for breakfast.'

'Don't change the subject,' said Daphne. 'Why did you say you had a kid?'

'I'm not trying to change the subject. It's just this thing I have. It's like, it's so adults-only it's not even called jam. It's called mahrm-ah-layd.'

Elli turned towards the sink, flicked on the tap and started filling the kettle. Daphne sat at the kitchen table in her dressing gown, loosely tied, barely concealing her boobs. Actually, scrap that. Daphne didn't have boobs, she had tits. 'Boobs are big and round and bouncy. Booooooobs. You've got boobs,' she'd say to Elli. 'I've got tits. Tits are lean and small. That's what I've got. Bits of tits.'

So Daphne, clad only in her dressing gown, which barely

concealed her tits, sat opposite Elli. Daphne rolled her first fag of the day. 'You could have just told him you're not that kind of girl.'

'But I am that kind of girl,' Elli grinned. 'That would be lying.'

'And telling him you had a kid isn't?'

'Yeah, true. Do you want a coffee?'

'Yes thanks.'

Elli had moved into Daphne's flat six months ago. Daphne had lived there originally with her boyfriend who used to be called Rob. Or Robbie. Or Babe. Or Hon. Now he was called, simply, 'The Bastard'. Ever since Daphne had walked in and found him in a cliché with some slut from his work, she had tossed in the pet names for a pet-rat name, and 'The Bastard' had instantly come to mind. Sometimes, because variety is the spice of life, she'd call him 'The Fucking Bastard', or 'The Arsehole', or 'The Prick', but as a general rule, he was referred to as 'The Bastard'. By Daphne. By all her friends. By her workmates. By some of his workmates. By people who didn't even know him but had heard the story through friends of friends. But most of all, most consistently, guaranteed, all the time, by Daphne.

Sweet Daphne, who looked like the flower she was named after. Delicate. Fragile. With skin like perfectly buffed petals. An only-there-for-the-spring-type feel to her. Short, wispy hair, dyed magenta, that lent her a fairy-at-the-end-of-the-garden-type edge. And a wistful, tiny body. Then Daphne, the wan little flower, the rare bloom, would laugh till she snorted, or tell Elli that 'The Bastard' had called again and she'd told him to jam it up his arse, and she didn't seem like a tenuous flower clinging to the end of a stem. She seemed like some shit-kicking bouganvillea, tangling her way through life, there for season after season, getting stronger and more in your face the longer she was left to her own devices.

'Besides, he was too young for me,' said Elli.

'How old was he?'

'I don't know. About twenty-five. Twenty-six maybe.'

'So?'

'I don't know. And he was a bit, I can't put my finger on it, shallow or something.'

Like the way he'd backed off as soon as she'd mentioned having a kid. Not that that had surprised her. It was why she'd said it. It had seemed easier than saying she wasn't ready yet. That she didn't really want to be with anyone at the moment because she was still hung up on Ben. Saying she had a kid seemed like a shortcut to the same result. But he might have surprised her. He might not have minded that she was a mother. He might have said, in his hot-chocolate-with-marshmallow voice 'that's okay'. After all, not all guys are scared off by the mention of a kid. Take Ben, for example. He was with Kate now, and she had a kid. It didn't seem to bother him. Not like it bothered Elli.

She just couldn't understand how Ben could dump her because she was 'getting too heavy' and then start going out with someone who had a kid. I mean, didn't having a kid instantly make it heavy? Surely a mum and a kid are heavier than just one single girl. A set of scales would be enough to prove that theory correct.

And she hadn't been getting 'heavy' with him anyway. She'd just had normal girlfriend/boyfriend expectations. She probably shouldn't have gotten so angry when he didn't call. But she was worried about him. Worried that something had happened to him. Like, another woman, for example. And when he wanted to go out with the boys, that was fine, but she just thought he was seeing them a bit too often. It was hardly heavying to explain what she wanted out of the relationship. Sure, maybe she shouldn't have cried about it for as long and as loudly as she had, maybe that was going too far, but she'd been upset. She couldn't help it.

'You know, sometimes I don't mind shallow,' Daphne said.

'Yeah? Why not?'

'Well, if you know it's never going to go anywhere, but if you just want a bit of fun, shallow can be just the ticket.'

It had been awful when Ben had told Elli he wanted to split. She had sensed it was coming, but she didn't know what she was doing wrong. She didn't know why he was distancing himself from her. It was like he kept setting tests for her, only she didn't know how to pass them because she didn't know what the right answers were. She didn't even know what the questions were, and the tests got longer and longer until they were lasting for days and then finally he had said 'it's not working', and she didn't know why. She'd told him they could work it out, how good they were together, how he would be making a mistake if he left her, but he didn't listen to any of it. He'd gone already, even though he was sitting right there, and she didn't know how to get him to come back. She'd hated pleading with him to give her another chance, but she felt sure that if they'd stayed together, things would have been different. She would have known there were tests she was expected to pass, she would have tried extra hard, and they'd still be Elli-and-Ben. But instead, he'd just said he wanted her out, maybe she could move in with her parents for a few weeks until she found somewhere else, and it had been humiliating and embarrassing and as if she would want to move in with them. She couldn't think of anything worse.

'Although,' said Daphne, 'I agree that as a general rule shallow is not the go. Like that guy Paul I went out with the other night. He was deeply shallow. Intensely shallow. Only talked about himself, didn't want to talk about me at all. And let's be honest, we all know which conversation would have been more interesting.'

Ben was always interesting to talk to. Never boring or shallow or self-absorbed. Although, he did talk about his music a fair bit. And the band. But that was interesting. Sometimes it was a bit boring, but generally it was interesting. What gigs they were getting. How many people were at each one. What song he was writing at any particular time. What mood he was trying to achieve. Different styles the band was starting to explore. What response they got from each song. When someone he didn't know recognised him at the supermarket.

Actually, he talked a shit-load about his music, but it was more a case of him just being really enthusiastic and focused and keen. And knowing what he thought and who he was and what he wanted. And what he didn't want. Like Elli. He hadn't wanted Elli anymore. He'd wanted her for a while, but then he didn't want her anymore. She didn't suit him anymore. She wasn't part of who he was anymore. So he'd ditched her. Just like that. Set a test, marked her incorrect, and dumped her. She wasn't even a D. She was a definite E for fail. E for Elli. How appropriate. She probably hadn't even gotten one tick-box right. They had all been wrong. Every single one of them. All wrong. Just like her.

'Are you okay?' Daphne asked.

'Yeah.'

'You've just gone a bit quiet all of a sudden.'

'No. I'm fine.'

'You're not thinking about Ben are you?'

'Ben? No, I haven't thought about him for ages.'

To be honest, she was even boring herself now, the way she kept obsessing over Ben. It didn't matter what she was doing, where she was, who she was with, Ben was there. It wasn't even like she wanted to think about him anymore. She wanted to *not-think* about him. She so wanted to not-think about him. But he was always there. It was like she had no control over her mind. Like her mind had turned into HAL and commandeered the craft. She'd make a firm decision not to think about Ben, but then HAL would say, 'I'm sorry, Dave, but we are going to think about Ben. I'm going to put these images of Ben up on the screen and you're going to watch them. Here's Ben getting dressed in the morning. Look at the clothes he's wearing. See how good those pants look on him. And here's another one of Ben, lying next to you. Remember his chest? Remember?' and Elli would be turning her head away 'No, I'm over him' and HAL would persist, his monotonous voice saying, 'I'm sorry, Dave, but you're not over him until I say you're over him.'

'You know,' Elli said to Daphne, not thinking of Ben, not thinking of Ben, not thinking of Ben, 'I had a bit of a *Sliding Doors*-type moment when I watched Minnow walk off last night.'

'In what way?'

'I just wondered what would have happened if I hadn't said I had a kid. If we'd kept kissing. If I'd gone back to his place. He might have been my soul mate and then I fucked it up because I said I had a kid. It's just possible that now I'll die an early and painful death by being knocked over by a car.'

'She didn't die in the car accident. She died when she fell down the stairs.'

'Did she? I don't remember. Anyway, the point is, I watched him walk off, and I kind of wondered if I'd done the wrong thing. He might have been my destiny.'

Probably not though, considering Ben was.

'No. If he's your destiny, it'll happen. You'll meet him again and it'll be on.'

'But it won't be on, because he thinks I've got a kid.'

'Well then, it wasn't meant to be.'

'But what if it was.'

'Then it'll happen.'

'But it can't.'

'So it won't.'

Elli looked at Daphne. 'Are you sure?'

'Definitely.'

Chapter 3

Real estate agents rarely get past number three on the Richter scale of honesty. But if Minnow was a real estate agent, he'd be different. He wouldn't bullshit anyone. He'd tell it as it is. And if he was writing about the reception he was sitting in at that very moment, he'd have written something along the lines of: 'Very average office. In need of total overhaul. A dump, having been given a quick lick of paint and wooden laminate wall dividers in the sixties, maybe seventies.'

Minnow sat in this dinosaur, waiting to meet Warren. Warren Bourke, Human Resources Manager. His appointment was for 11:30, but apparently Warren had wagged telling-the-time at school because it was now quarter to twelve and Minnow was still sitting in reception.

It hadn't seemed like the worst idea in the world, when he'd seen this job advertised, but now he was having second thoughts. In hindsight, it was the ritual of looking for a job that had appealed to him, not the actual gaining of labour. The process of hauling the wad of 'Employment' out of Saturday's *Age*, flicking it open like a corporate cowboy, smoothing it out onto the bar in front of him, and studying it formguide-like, pen in hand. It had seemed like a good thing to do. Sitting at Crush, waiting for Doug to arrive, the morning after the night before. Looking for a job seemed to have a vaguely interesting ring to it.

Crush used to be an old garage in Elwood, in Ormond Road. It hadn't been a very popular garage, but fuck me, it was a shit-hot bar. Concrete floors, paint-chipped walls, old petrol company calendars of girls with tits that looked like they had a full 60 pounds of air in them. That's 60 pounds, each tit. Pneumatic nymphs. The outside hadn't been painted since its glory days in the car-servicing industry, and an old Castrol logo was peeling off the big roll-a-door at the front. There was a kind of retro, grunge, post-modern, industrial, blue-collar, slutty-sex-calendars-type feel to the place.

So he'd read Saturday's employment section while he waited for Doug to show, and now he was reading *New Idea* while he waited for Warren Bourke, Human Resources Manager, to show.

Minnow looked at his watch. He was going to leave if Warren didn't front soon.

Minnow sat on the grey-blue 1970s couch in reception, wearing his grey-blue three-button 1950s op-shop suit. It had that been-in-someone-else's-wardrobe-for-years smell to it, that bit-tight-under-the-arms-but-not-so's-you'd-notice-it feel. He'd caught sight of himself as he walked past a shop window and yeah, he looked sharp, in a retro kind of a Steve-McQueen-if-Steve-McQueen-had-ever-worn-a-suit-type way. If he was a girl, he'd fuck him.

Five to twelve. Minnow had had some luminous ideas in the past, but getting a job wasn't one of them. Sure, he needed the cash, sure, he had this most massive Visa bill, but working, especially in a dump like this, might have to wait a while.

He was going to give Warren Bourke, Human Resources Manager, five more minutes, and then he was outta there.

He watched the receptionist answer the phone, 'Radio 625 FM, Mona speaking'. Two things Minnow thought. First. Weren't radio stations supposed to be groovy? Second. What sort of parents called their kid Mona? She was about 19, looked like she'd never had sex in her life, but she was called Moaner. If he worked here, he'd definitely have to fuck her. She probably hated her folks for giving her a name like that. Parents. You couldn't trust them.

Which reminded him. That chick from the other night — Elli. He still couldn't believe she had a kid, that *she* was a mother. I mean, he had a mum. His friends had mums. He saw mums out on the street every day, pushing prams, screeching at kids, wearing bad clothes and worse hair. He knew what mums looked like. He didn't get erections over mothers.

But that girl from Wednesday night, she was so rootable, it was a total spinout. And her kiss. Mothers don't kiss like that. Mothers give pecks. Mothers are thinking about putting on another load of washing, how the floor needs a mop, what's for dinner. But Elli, she wasn't thinking about the floor. Except maybe to fuck on. When Minnow had kissed her mouth he had wondered how her nipple would taste. He imagined swilling her nipple around with his tongue. Licking it, savouring the flavour. Like some kind of a fine tit connoisseur. He'd wanted to lift her red top up, push her back against the car and work his way with his mouth down to her nipples. Then, he would have slowly peeled her pants off, right there, on Collins Street, and . . .

'Hi, Simon? I'm Warren. Warren Bourke. Sorry I got caught up.'

Minnow stood up. 'Fuck, Warren. Your timing is totally shitful. I've been sitting here for 25 minutes, but you wait until I'm enjoying the most massive erection before you come and get me.'

No, actually, he said, 'Hi Warren. That's fine,' and shook Warren's hand.

Minnow followed Warren Bourke past The Moaner at reception, his walloping penis standing to attention the whole way down the corridor. Minnow directed flaccid thoughts of fat old grandmas down his pants. Although, judging by the way Warren Bourke was mincing down the corridor ahead of him, he'd probably be thrilled and delighted if he knew that Minnow was following behind with an erection.

Warren Bourke, Human Resources Manager, turned to Minnow.

'I'm afraid there's a meeting in the boardroom, so we'll have to use my office.'

'Sure. No problem.'

Warren ushered Minnow in. Minnow looked around. There was something fascinating about other people's offices. It was like walking into their bedroom. Minnow always enjoyed spending time in someone's office when they weren't there, looking through their things, seeing what they were working on, going through their drawers. But Warren's office was so beige, so deadly dull, it wasn't even fun to speculate what was in those filing cabinets. Probably just files.

They both sat down. On the wall behind Warren's head was a poster with the words 'You don't have to be crazy to work here, but it helps.'

Says it all, doesn't it?

'That's a classic poster, Warren.'

Apparently Warren Bourke, Human Resources Manager,

had wagged sarcasm at school as well as telling the time, because the tone of Minnow's voice went sailing over Warren's head, and all he caught were the words, dropping in order, past his 100 per cent acrylic jumper and landing on the lap of his cheap grey flannel pants.

Warren looked behind his shoulder, as if he needed to be reminded of the great wit he had Blu-Tacked to the wall. He smiled modestly. 'Do you like it?'

'Oh yeah.'

They say if you can fake sincerity, you've got it made. Looks like Minnow had it made.

'And you know,' Warren chuckled, 'I think it's true. We are all a bit crazy. All of us. The whole crew.'

Warren Bourke, Human Resources Manager, smiled at Minnow. Minnow smiled back. Crew? What sort of fucking loser says 'crew'? He wondered if Warren still lived with his mother. Probably. He certainly wouldn't be living with his wife or girlfriend. Or boyfriend. Not with a personality like that. And how about that hair of Warren's? There was a very high pube factor in that hair. Probably an 8. Maybe even a 9. It was the sort of hair that should have remained firmly tucked inside a pair of boxer shorts, but had somehow managed to creep out of Warren's underwear and was now snuggled up in a clump on top of his head. Warren didn't seem to have noticed.

'The office has a great feel to it,' said Minnow.

Minnow could see he would have some excellent sport if he worked here with Warren Bourke, Human Resources Manager.

'You know, Simon, it does. They may not be the most glam-orous offices,' (you're right on the fucking money with that one, Warren) 'but everyone here is great. And in fact, the person we're looking for would need to be able to fit in here, because we all get on so well.'

'Well, that's exactly what I'm after. To be part of a team.' Sometimes Minnow even surprised himself. He was so good at this sort of bullshit.

'You know,' said Warren, 'I have a feeling you'd really get on well here. Tell me a bit about yourself. What have you done?'

Well, Warren, I've done cocaine, ecstasy, GHB, trips, speed, mushrooms, dope of course, and smoked a bit of smack. How about you? 'I did a bit of sales while I was living overseas, but my main experience before I left Melbourne was working at IBM.'

'Really? They've got a great training program there apparently.'

'Yeah. I was Salesman of the Month on a few occasions, actually.'

'Wow. You must have been a real asset. So, why don't you go back to IBM, now that you've returned from overseas?'

Well, let me see. Partly because that stuff about Salesman of the Month is crap, but mainly because I fucked the General Manager's secretary on his desk at the Christmas party and when he found out, he wasn't super impressed.

'Look, I could, Warren. But I'd feel a bit like I was going backwards. Do you know what I mean? I've been there, I know how they operate, I think it's a great company with some fantastic techniques, but I want to move forward and apply those skills in a different environment. Also, I'd rather work in a smaller place, with the opportunity of moving up more quickly.'

Omigod. What was he saying? He was actually sounding like he really wanted the job, and really wanted to put in the hours, and really wanted to work in this crusty old office. Iqbal! As in Asif Iqbal, the Pakistani cricketer. As in, as if. As if he wanted to work here. Sure, he needed a job. Sure, he needed money. Sure, it had sounded good in the paper. But the reality didn't measure up. It was a crap office, with a particularly annoying Human Resources Manager, and a fair chance that the rest of the 'crew' were nuff-nuffs as well. Besides, he still hadn't caught up with all his friends, and there were heaps of new bars he hadn't been to yet. He didn't have time to be working as well.

'Yes, well there's plenty of movement around this place. In fact, the person you'd be replacing is now the Sales Manager.'

'Great.'

There were a couple of other jobs he'd circled in the paper. He'd have to give them a call. In a week or two. A month at the latest. He just wasn't ready to work. Although the money here probably wouldn't be bad. And he'd shit it all over the other people who worked here. The thing was, he wanted cash, not a career. Not at the moment. He was still in holiday mode. He hadn't had a proper job the whole time he was away. Building work, bar work, telesales. But not full-time. Just to get a bit of extra dosh. Cash him up for his side trips. He didn't want to start working full-time. Not yet. He'd probably started looking for jobs too soon. He shouldn't have rung.

'So you'd be available to start straight away, I assume.'

He'd look again this Saturday in the *Age*, but this time he'd use his smarts and circle part-time work instead. Maybe bar work. He'd never had so much sex as when he worked in that bar in London. Yeah, bar work would be good. Although the pay's shit. That's the piss-off about working in hospitality. Fun. Good drugs as a general rule. But shit pay. So even though the drugs were better, you couldn't have as many of them. The thing is to work part-time, get paid well, party hard, fuck a lot, sleep in, take lots of drugs, buy a motorbike, and buy a car. Actually, what he needed was a job with a car. He didn't want to pay for one, he wanted to be given one.

'There's a car with this position isn't there, Warren?'

'Of course.'

Hmm. Tick that box.

'And what money are we talking?'

'Around sixty-five, including commission.'

Yeah, that's good. That'd be nice.

So, on the plus side, there's a company car and a fat wad of cash each month. On the down side, the offices are really bad, and it's full-time hours. And Warren. Warren he could cope with. The offices he couldn't really give a shit about. But the hours.

'It's a full-time job isn't it?'

'Yes. We've got a couple of women working part-time, but most of our reps are full-time.'

That'd be right. Pump out a couple of kids and you can work whatever hours you like. Cushy job, easy hours, just because you've got a vagina. None of the guys with kids probably worked part-time. It was discrimination. Guys couldn't work part-time because they didn't have a womb. That was basically what it came down to. Part-time work? I'm afraid you're only eligible if you've given birth. It was about time a few men put their hand up and said, 'No, I want the cushy job too. I want a job where I only work a few hours a day, where I can "pop off" to pick the kids up from school. I want the job where I need to be home for the electrician. You know what? I want what she's got.'

Minnow looked at Warren Bourke, Human Resources Manager, and was suddenly struck, really hard, in the stomach, with an absolutely brilliant idea. He leaned forward and put his elbow on Warren's desk. He smiled.

'So you've got a few working mums here?'

'Yes, we do.'

'How does it work?'

'I must say, it works really well. I was a bit sceptical at first, but there have been no problems.' Warren paused. Then he said, 'In fact, it's good.'

Minnow rubbed his lip thoughtfully.

'That's great, Warren, because actually I've got a little tyke myself' (good, matey, blokey, dadsy word). 'Didn't see him while I was overseas, but now I'm back and his mum has shot through and left him with me, and I'd like to be able to pick him up from school each day.'

Warren's Adam's apple moved up, then back down.

'You are an equal-opportunity employer here, aren't you Warren?'

'Well, yes, of course we are.'

'Great.'

Minnow sat back in his chair and smiled. Fuck. He was bloody good.

Chapter 4

It was Saturday afternoon, about 2:30.

Daphne and Elli were smack-bang in the middle of a pyjama day. You know. A pyjama day. In case you're not familiar with pyjama days: as a general rule, you don't realise you're having a pyjama day until about 2:00 p.m., when you look down and notice you're still in your pj's — you haven't had a shower, you haven't brushed your teeth and you haven't moved off the couch pretty much all day. Pyjama days cannot be planned. You cannot say 'let's have a pyjama day tomorrow'. You can't pretend, or try to make yourself feel like having a pyjama day. You arrive there completely by accident. It's a day you trip into and don't even realise it's happening until it's nearly finished. A list of things to do on a pyjama day: Watch a video. Watch the midday movie (preferably Doris Day with Rock Hudson, Elvis, or Bing and Bob, but you gotta be lucky). Read the newspaper. Read trashy magazines. Listen to music. Have a joint. Eat toasted sandwiches. Drink wine, or vodka and tonic. Kip on the couch, but only for a short time — it's most important that your pj's aren't used for sleeping on a pyjama day.

The most popular option, of course, is the smoke joint, watch midday movie, read newspaper, read trashy mags, smoke another joint, veg on the couch, don't answer the phone, eat toasted cheese sambos and don't brush teeth route. That is the road most travelled, and the route that Elli and Daphne chose for the duration of their pyjama day. Elli in her singlet and pyjama pants, Daphne in her dressing gown, loosely tied.

Daphne always wore her dressing gown loosely tied. She figured she was only going to be in it for a short amount of time, so there wasn't much point spending the time and effort necessary to tie it up properly. Because if you tied it up properly, that involved tying the little strings on the *inside* of the dressing gown, before you tied the belt on the *outside*. Too much like hard work.

Anyway, Elli lay on the couch under the window, reading trashy mags, telly on. Daphne cosied into the lounge chair, reading the newspaper, feet on the coffee table, hiking socks on. She needed the hiking socks for walking to the kitchen and back. Cold floor.

'It says here,' said Daphne, 'that they did this survey, and people who won Tattslotto were just as happy, six months later, as people who had been involved in a major car accident, or someone who had cancer.'

'Really?'

'Yeah.'

'How does that work?'

'It's like, people who are happy will be happy whether they win Tattslotto or have a car accident, and people who are unhappy will be unhappy no matter what.'

'Right. I think I'd prefer to win Tattslotto if I had the choice though.'

'Same.'

Elli wondered whether that applied to relationships as well. Whether she didn't really need Ben to be happy. If she didn't need Ben to be happy, if it was up to her, that would be a real relief. It would mean that she wouldn't need to keep thinking about Ben all the time. It would mean that Ben, oh fuck, she was thinking about Ben again . . .

Silence. Daphne reading the newspaper, Elli reading trashy mags. The occasional turning of the page from Daphne. The flick, flick, flick of Elli hoeing into her *Who Weekly*.

Daphne put down the newspaper and stood up.

'Toasted sambo?' she asked.

'Oooh yeah.'

'Cheese and tomato?'

'Yum,' said Elli. 'Do you want me to help?'

'No, I'm right.'

That was good, because Elli honestly couldn't be fucked getting off the couch. She went back to her *Who*.

When reading trashy mags, there are a number of different reading styles you can choose from. You can do the old, trusty from-the-back-to-the-front. Or, you can start-at-the-beginning-and-go-all-the-way-to-the-end. Alternatively, you can flick-through-and-then-go-back-again-starting-with-what-look-like-the-most-interesting-stories. Elli was, and always had been, a start-at-the-beginning-and-go-all-the-way-to-the-end-type girl. She liked to read a story and not know what the picture on the next page was going to be, because if she knew what the picture on the next page was going to be, she might flick to that instead, and miss out on some vital piece of trash on the page she was on at the moment. Her favourite articles in trashy mags were, of course, the ones featuring the main

Hollywood players, followed closely by other famous people, so long as they weren't politicians, then the snapshots of famous people with captions which tried to be funny, fourth favourite was feng shui tips for you at home, next, astrology and what the week holds in store for you, and finally, stories of tragedies that happen to ordinary people. But certainly, the clear winners were the stories about Hollywood — the clothes, the excess, the houses, the cars, the turmoil, the gossip, the parties — which were probably all bullshit, but she read every word anyway.

'Omigod,' she called out to Daphne.

'What?' Daphne called from the kitchen.

'You should see the house Brad and Jennifer have bought.'

'What's it like?' Daphne called back.

'It's full on. You'll have to have a look. The pool is out of control.'

Silence. Flick. Silence. Flick.

'It's nice that Hugo Collings is still with his wife, isn't it?'

'Who?'

'Hugo and his wife.'

'Yeah, that's good.'

Silence. Flick. Silence. Flick. Daphne came back in. Toasted cheese and tomato sambos all round.

'You know, Gwyneth shits me.'

'Same.'

'She always wears really nice clothes though.'

'Yeah. And boyfriends.'

'Yeah. She wears really nice boyfriends.'

Silence. Flick. Silence. Flick.

'Have a look at Catherine and Michael toddling off to the supermarket. Seriously, I'd wear that to a party.'

Daphne had a look at the photo Elli was pointing to. 'Yeah, she always looks good.'

'If they gave me maybe ten per cent of what they earn, I'd be happy and they'd still be filthy rich.'

'How much would that be?'

'I don't know,' said Elli. 'Say she earns a million dollars per movie, and he probably earns ten million dollars, together that's eleven million dollars. So, if they gave me ten per cent of even just one movie they each made, I'd have one million, one hundred thousand dollars.'

'Fuck. That's not bad. Except they would never do it.'

'Maybe I could become a movie star and make a million dollars each time I got out of bed,' said Elli.

'Or a supermodel,' said Daphne.

'Yeah, I could definitely do that. Or maybe the lead singer of a really famous band, like say, the Rolling Stones.'

'Except Mick's got that gig.'

'Yeah, but he's getting on. He might be wanting to hand over the reins.'

'True. Can you sing?'

'As well as he can.' Daphne laughed.

'What about marrying money? That'd be easy.'

'Ugh. The problem is, marrying money usually means marrying old and ugly.'

'True,' said Elli.

Silence. Flick.

'Not in here though. If you're a movie star you get to marry another movie star.'

'Then you go back to having to be a movie star in the first place,' Daphne pointed out.

'Hmm,' said Elli.

'And, the movie star you married would probably be gay, which is not really a quality to be desired in a husband.'

'Yeah, you're right.'

Silence. Flick. Silence. Flick.

Elli said, 'What would you rather marry? Rich, old, ugly and straight or rich, young, handsome and gay?'

'Neither.'

'But if you didn't have a choice. If you had to marry one or the other.'

'What's their personality like?'

'Um. Okay.'

'Well, I suppose in that case, if one of them's got quite a good personality . . .'

'I didn't say "quite a good personality", I said "okay". In fact, they're both a bit boring.'

'Oh. Well, in that case, I think I'd go for young, rich, handsome and gay,' said Daphne. 'At least that way you'd get to go to all the fun parties. If you went old, rich, ugly and straight, with an average personality, you'd go to boring parties, plus you'd have to sleep with some wrinkly old piece of blanket as well, and that'd be no good.'

'Yeah. That'd be gross.'

Silence. Flick.

'How about poor and happy.'

'If I had to. What about you?'

'Begrudgingly.'

Silence. Flick. Silence. Flick.

'If there was absolutely no alternative.'

Silence. Flick. Silence. Flick.

'Rich, happy and in love would be better though.'

'Absolutely.'

Silence. Flick. Silence. Flick.

'You know,' said Elli, putting the magazine on her lap, 'if a rich person gave you even one per cent, say Catherine and Michael gave us one per cent of their earnings, we would be more than happy, and they seriously wouldn't even notice it was gone.'

'Yeah. Except, why do you think they're rich? What if they're tightarses? They wouldn't just hand their money out to someone they don't even know.'

'Mmm.'

Silence. Flick. Silence. Flick. Slow turn from Daphne.

'But they do give their money away,' said Elli. 'To like, charities and the arts and stuff. If we were a charity, we'd probably get a whopping fat cheque.'

'Yeah. Except we're not a charity.'

'No.'

Silence.

'But you know,' said Elli, 'if we asked, they might give us something. You never know.'

'What do you mean?'

'You know, if we just asked them straight out for money. They might just give it to us.'

'And why would they do that?'

'I don't know. Maybe we caught them on a good day. Or maybe they're really generous people, except no-one apart from charities ever thinks to ask them for money. And that's why they only ever give their money to charities, because they don't know who else wants it.'

Daphne nodded her head. 'Yeah, probably,' she said, in a tone which really said, 'yeah, probably never'. She went back to reading her newspaper.

After quite a time of silence, Daphne looked over at Elli. 'What are you doing?' asked Daphne.

'Nothing.'

'Exactly. Why?'

'I was just thinking that we could write a letter, asking for money. Not a charity letter, just a letter, straight, saying we're two young girls who don't earn heaps of money, but would like to travel overseas, and would they care to donate to our trip.'

Daphne kept reading. 'I'm sure they'd love to.'

'I mean, they probably wouldn't.' Silence. No flick. 'But they might. They might think, "That's good. They're not bull-shitting us, making up some story. They're just being really up front about it."'

'They might,' said Daphne. As in, they definitely wouldn't.

Elli got off the lounge and looked down at Daphne.

'Have we got any paper anywhere?' she asked.

'Yeah,' said Daphne, 'there's a layout pad in my bedroom.'

'Can I grab it?'

'Sure.'

Elli came back in. She sat up, back straight, on the couch.

Daphne looked at her from around the side of her news-paper. 'What are you doing?'

'I'm writing a letter.'

Daphne put down the newspaper. 'What are you saying?'

'Dear Mr Packer . . .'

'Good so far,' Daphne giggled.

'We are two young girls . . .'

'Young, attractive girls.'

'Do you think I should write that?'

'No. As if. I'm kidding.'

'. . . two young girls, who aren't earning much money . . .'

'Are broke.'

'. . . who are broke, but who are very keen to go over-seas.'

'Do you think we should say we want to go overseas? I mean, he might think it's great that we want to travel, but he might not want to pay for it.'

'Mmm. Okay. How about this: ". . . who are broke, but who don't want to be anymore."'

'Yeah, that's good. I like it. It's open-ended.'

'We figure that if someone gave us a bit of a hand finan-cially . . .'

'Do you think "figure" is right?'

'How about "believe"?'

'Yeah, that's better.'

'. . . if someone gave us a bit of a hand financially, we could really do great things.'

'I like it. It's corny, but good.'

'We believe . . .'

'You've already used "believe".'

'We feel . . .'

'Good.'

'. . . that the amount we're talking would hardly be small change to you.'

'To someone of your immense wealth.'

'. . . to someone of your immense wealth.'

'Got to flatter him.'

'True. ". . . would hardly be small change to someone of your immense wealth, but for us, it would make a real dif-ference to our . . ."'

Silence.

'. . . circumstances.'

'Yep.'

'We are looking for a donation . . .'

'I'm not sure about "donation".'

'. . . benefactor . . .'

'Brilliant.'

'. . . to bestow? Bequeath?'

'How about "to subsidise"?'

'Yeah, that's not bad, ". . . to subsidise our . . . financial independence . . ."'

'You're good.'

'Thank you. ". . . to the value of $100,000."'

'Do you think that's enough?'

'I don't know.'

'I mean, it might be enough.'

'We don't want to ask for too much, otherwise he might not pay.'

'But we don't want to be too cheap, either.'

'No.'

'How about if we don't ask for any amount. How about if you write something like "whatever you think is a fair sum to get us on our feet"?'

'Yeah. Okay.'

'Because he might pay more than $100,000.'

'True. "Yours faithfully".'

'Do you think you should write something about, "next time you're in Melbourne, please feel free to drop by and say hello"?'

'Yeah, that might be a nice touch.'

It took them a while to write, nearly an entire week, but finally they were finished.

'Forty-five dollars in postage. Not bad for a potentially massive return on investment.'

'It's good. Even if we only get one reply.'

Mailed.

To Kerry Packer.

And ninety-nine others. The *BRW* list of the one hundred richest men and women in Australia.

Chapter 5

It took a lot to gobsmack Kate. A lot.

She'd been best friends with Minnow and Doug for about fifteen years now, so she wasn't gobsmacked easily. For example, there was the time when she had caught the tram home from school with Doug and Minnow (this was the year they had met). A lardarse housewife had glared at Doug and said to him, 'You know, if you stood up, you could give someone a seat,' and Doug smiled back at her and said, 'If you stood up, you could give two people a seat.' Kate had been gobsmacked then, admittedly, but she was only young at the time, and inexperienced at the workings of Doug and Minnow.

About six years ago (when she was older and wiser in the workings of Doug and Minnow, but not older and wiser in the workings of Elliot, her boyfriend of the time), Elliot had dumped her, leaving her with an 18-month-old baby called Lochie. So Minnow and Doug had put a hose through the window of Elliot's brand-new car, filled it up with water and spray-painted 'cunt' down both sides of it. Kate had laughed when she heard what they'd done, and you certainly couldn't call her condition gobsmacked (actually, she thought they were rather sweet to do it).

Even two weeks ago with that girl Jacinta or Janine or whatever her name was, even that didn't gobsmack Kate. Minnow had met this girl, Kate was pretty sure her name was Jacinta, at Marco's art exhibition.

'Call me,' she'd slurred at Minnow as he climbed out of her bed.

'That's the difference between guys and girls,' Minnow had said the next day to Kate and Doug, over a drink at Crush. 'Girls don't get the essence of a one-night stand. A one-night stand is for one night, hence the name. But girls think of it as the beginning of something. They don't see it as an end in itself. So they set themselves up for disappointment. They should adopt more of a male approach, more of "a fuck is a fuck not a relationship" type approach, don't you reckon, Doug?'

'Absolutely,' said Doug, rolling himself a fag.

'Don't worry, Minnow,' said Kate. 'I'm sure if they got to know you better, they'd adopt the even simpler "fuck-off" approach towards you, it's just that you never let them.'

Minnow grinned at Kate.

'I'll take that as a compliment,' he said.

'It's not meant to be,' said Kate, as she reached over for Doug's pack of tobacco. 'Can I have one of these?' she asked.

'Sure. Do you want me to roll it for you?'

'No, I'll give it a go.'

Minnow went on to tell them how Jacinta, yeah, that was her name, had fumbled around in the dark, looking for a pen and paper. Minnow stopped her.

'Don't write it down. Just tell it to me. I'll remember,' he had said. Which of course was perfect, because it meant that if he ever saw her again, he could say he was going to ring her, but couldn't remember the number.

'No you won't,' she had said.

'I will. I promise.'

'Promise?'

'Yes.'

'Scout's honour?'

'Yes.'

'Really?'

'Yes.'

'No you won't.'

'I will, alright? Just tell me. I'll remember. I've got a great memory.'

'Okay. It's easy. 9532 6969.'

Minnow had laughed. 'Well, I certainly should remember that.'

Jacinta had smiled in the darkness of her bedroom. 'You certainly should.'

And the thing was, he did. He couldn't get the stupid phone number out of his head. Driving home that night, 9532 6969. Going to sleep, 9532 6969. Waking up the next morning, 9532 6969. He couldn't get the fucking number out of his head.

'You've got to love a girl who has a sexual position for a phone number,' Doug said, taking a deep drag.

'So are you going to call?' Kate asked.

'Iqbal.'

'You should.'

'Why?'

'Because you said you would.'

'No I didn't. She told me to, but I didn't say I would. I said I'd remember her phone number, and I've done that, but I didn't say I'd call her.'

'No, I suppose not.'

Minnow ordered more beers, and a vodka and tonic for Kate.

'I just think it's mean not to call,' Kate said again. 'She'll feel really used. It's guys like you who give men a bad name.'

'What for?'

'For being users and not calling.'

'Hey, it's not like I'm the only one who was into it. She couldn't get her gear off fast enough.'

'Maybe, but . . .'

'In fact, I feel rather used myself. She just used me for sex.'

'Ha ha.'

'Well, what's the difference? We both used each other for sex.'

'But she was expecting it to go somewhere, and you always knew it was going nowhere.'

'I didn't know she was expecting it to go anywhere except the cot, until she told me to call her.'

'That's crap, Minnow.'

'What? So you think I should take her out because I feel sorry for her?'

'No. I just think, I don't know, at least if you took her out once she might not feel so used.'

'Do I get to have sex with her again?' Minnow asked.

'No. Not if it'd be another one-night stand.'

'Technically,' said Doug, 'I think you'd find it was a second-night stand.'

'Yeah, that's true,' said Minnow. 'And what's the traditional male stance on second-night stands?' he asked Doug.

'As a general rule,' said Doug, 'a second-night stand is viewed pretty much the same as a one-night stand. Although, there is more of a window of opportunity — from the girl's point of view — for it to become a verge-of-a-relationship-type thing. Just the very fact that you've made the phone call takes it past the one-night stand.'

Minnow took a swig of his beer.

'Dangerous territory, the second-night stand,' he said. 'Best avoided.'

Kate shook her head. 'You guys are pathetic,' she said.

More beer. Another vodka and tonic. Kate still bleating on about this 'poor girl'.

'Why don't you take her out, if you feel so sorry for her,' Minnow said to Kate.

'Maybe I will. And I'll explain to her why it's not a good idea to have one-night stands with bastards like you.'

'What sort of bastards should she have one-night stands with then?'

'Nice bastards.'

More beer. One more voddie. And then Doug said, 'Maybe *I'll* take her out.'

'Yeah, you should,' said Minnow. 'She's a goer.'

'Minnow,' said Kate, 'show a bit of respect.'

'Why? I didn't respect her before. Why should I respect her now?'

Kate punched Minnow in the arm.

'Ow.' He rubbed it for a minute, and then stopped rubbing as a sly grin slid into position.

'What?' asked Kate.

'Nothing,' said Minnow.

'No, what? What are you thinking?' she persisted.

'I was just thinking that it would be really funny if you rang,' he was talking to Doug now, 'and said you were me, and took her out. As me.'

Doug grinned. Kate shook her head.

'You can't do that,' she said.

'Why not?'

'Because I think she might notice Doug's not you. And his accent may tip her off. And besides, it's mean.'

'No it's not,' said Minnow. 'It's doing what you suggested.'

'What I suggested?'

'Yeah. You said I should take her out so she doesn't feel used. I don't want to take her out, I'm not into her. But Doug can take her out — she won't know he's not me because she was totally trashed. And we look similar.'

Kate looked at Minnow and Doug. They did look similar. Both had blond hair. Both good-looking. Similar build, although Minnow was taller than Doug. The voice would be about the only thing that might clue the poor girl in to the fact that the Minnow she was having dinner with was not the Minnow she'd had sex with a few nights before. Doug was originally from America, and even though his accent wasn't all that strong anymore, it was still there.

Minnow looked at Kate.

'That way she won't feel used. I'm only trying to do the right thing,' he said.

'Fuck off, you are not.'

'What's she like?' asked Doug, leaning forward.

'She's a babe. And she's got a cool flat.'

'If she's such a babe,' asked Kate, stirring her v & t with a straw, 'why don't you want to take her out again?'

'You know, I might have if she hadn't told me to call her. As soon as she said that, it was like she was some kind of desperado.'

'Well, maybe she asked you to call because you didn't ask for her phone number.'

'Well, maybe I didn't ask for her phone number because I wasn't interested in calling her.'

'Yeah, I know, but some girls are just like that, you know. They like to assert themselves.'

'Pushy.'

'No, not pushy. Okay, assert wasn't the right word. They're, I don't know . . .' Kate put her finger to her chin and tapped, as if trying to knock out the appropriate word. 'Keen.'

'Desperate.'

'Piss off, not desperate. Keen's not the right word either. You know, it's not fair. You guys say it's fine for a girl to call, that it's okay for the girl to do the chasing. That you like it. And then when the girl is up front and says she'd like you to call, you say she's pushy or desperate.'

'Your point?'

Kate rested her chin in her hand. 'I'm not sure.'

'So what do you think?' Minnow asked Doug.

'Yeah, I think it's an excellent idea.'

'Excuse me?' Kate asked, perking up. 'You think what's excellent?'

'Taking this chick out and saying I'm Minnow.'

'You're not doing that.'

'Oh yeah, sure I am.'

And he did. He rang that poor girl right there and then, and took her out the next night.

'Great sex,' Doug had said the next day. And that was it. That was the last Kate had heard of poor Jacinta. But even then, she wasn't gobsmacked. Having been best friends with Minnow and Doug for most of her life, she was aware of how low they could go.

The month before, when Minnow told her about his new job at the radio station, she wasn't gobsmacked.

'Congratulations,' said Kate, giving him a hug. 'That'll be ace fun. Waiter. Champagne for my friend,' she'd said, clicking her fingers at Michael as he walked past.

'Bar service, luvvie,' Michael said with a fuck-you finger held up in her direction. The staff at Crush had such an attitude problem.

'So when do you start?' she asked when she came back from the bar.

'Monday.'

'Great.'

'Nine till three each day.'

'Really? Wow, that's great. Brilliant hours. How come?'

'I said I had to pick up my kid from school.'

'What kid?'

'My kid.'

Kate pushed her glass of champagne to the side as if it was tap water.

'But you don't have a kid.'

'Yes, I know, but they don't know that. I've told them that I'm a single dad; that my ex dumped the kid on my doorstep a couple of days after I came back from overseas.'

Kate looked blankly at Minnow. Okay, okay, she was gobsmacked. She couldn't think of a thing to say. So Minnow continued on with his story.

'I told them she was a smack addict, and she just upped and left the other day, leaving me and the poor little kid to struggle along together. And I said that naturally I wanted to do the right thing by him, and pick him up from school each day. They said it'd be bonus. Heaps of mums do it.' Minnow took a swig of his champagne and clinked it against Kate's glass, which was still sitting, cold and lonely, on the table in front of her. 'So now, we can be single mums together, sort of,' he said.

Kate shook her head as if to focus her hearing and her speech. Finally, she said, 'So how old did you say the little boy was?'

'Eight.'

'But what if they check?'

'Check what?'

'Whether or not you've got a kid?'

'Who with?'

'I don't know. The Bureau of Statistics. The Government.'

'They never check. I don't think one thing I've ever bull-shitted about in a job interview has ever been checked. I said I was Salesman of the Month too.'

'What? At IBM?'

'Yeah.'

Kate burst out laughing. 'Omigod. You're unbelievable.'

'Thank you.'

Minnow put Kate's glass back in her hand and winked at her.

'Skol,' he said, and slugged back the rest of his champagne. 'I'm just going to put a couple of photos of Lochie on my desk . . .'

'Lochie. My Lochie? You are not.'

'Oh yes. I've already gone through and selected a couple.'

'No way.'

'Yes way.'

'Excuse me, but you're not putting pictures of my son on your desk as if he's your kid. What if I know someone there?

Then, not only will they think I've dumped my kid, they'll also think I'm a junkie, and that I've had sex with you at some stage in my life. Ugh.'

Minnow smiled at her.

'You should be so lucky.'

Kate shook her head.

'Besides,' Minnow said, 'I doubt you'd know anyone who works in this place. It's radio at its most suburban.'

'Well, that's not the point. I don't want you to pretend Lochie is your son. Use one of your sister's kids.'

'I can't. She's only got girls. I said I had a boy.'

'Say you made a mistake.'

'Sure. "Sorry Warren. You know how I said I had a boy, well, I had a good look last night at bathtime and gadzooks, she's a girl." I don't think so.'

Kate took a sip of her champagne and shrugged her shoulders. 'Fine, use his photo. I think it's bad karma, but it's your life.'

In fact, once she'd gotten used to the whole idea of him pretending to have a kid, it didn't smack her gob anymore. She almost considered it vintage Minnow.

But yesterday, when Minnow asked whether he could take Lochie on a picnic with the receptionist from his new work and whether it'd be okay if Lochie called him 'Dad' for the day, Kate was well and truly smacked in the gob.

'You can't be serious,' she said.

'What?'

Kate stood up and went into the kitchen to make a coffee.

'I'm not even going to have this conversation.'

'Come on Kate, I need to.'

'Piss off.'

'No, seriously. I've told Mona I'm bringing him. It's a done deal. She really wants to meet him.'

Kate remained resolutely silent in the kitchen.

'This whole single dad thing, you know,' he continued, 'it really turns her on.'

'Bad luck.'

'Please.'

Kate stood at the doorway to the kitchen.

'No. I can't believe you're asking me. What sort of fucked-up mother do you think I am?'

'Alright, I won't get him to call me Dad. Plenty of kids call their parents by their first name anyway.'

'You're not taking him.'

'Why?'

'You're just not. If you want to bullshit about being a single dad, that's your business. Lochie's photo, fine. But don't ever expect to take him into work with you, or to any work functions, or to meet anyone from your work.'

'Kate,' said Minnow, grinning.

But Kate didn't smile. Her mouth remained a grim line on her angry face.

'I'm serious Minnow. I'm actually really pissed off with you.'

Minnow leaned back into the couch and folded his arms across his chest.

'What for?'

'You don't really expect me to answer that.'

'Yeah, I do. I won't take Lochie, no problem. I don't know what you're getting so upset about.'

'Don't make out like I'm being unreasonable. What you've asked is morally wrong, and the fact that you honestly thought I'd be fine with it is really insulting.'

'Why?'

Kate looked at Minnow, her face screwed up as if she was trying to see through some kind of a fog. Then she shrugged her shoulders. 'No. No reason. It's just, I find that you thinking I would let you take Lochie out on a date with some bimbo from your work, call you Dad, and pretend that his mum, me, has run off and dumped him with you, I don't know, I find it all a bit tasteless. Call me overly sensitive.'

'Yeah, okay.'

Kate walked over to Minnow and pointed her finger at him, 'Dead set Minnow, if you think I'm being overly sensitive, then you're more fucked up than I thought you were.'

Minnow pulled Kate onto the couch and put his arm around her. 'So does that mean yes?'

'No it doesn't.'

She got back up off the couch.

'Do you want a coffee?' she asked.

'Yes please,' he said.

Kate walked back into the kitchen.

'So what do I say to Mona?' Minnow asked, trying to make Kate feel like the imminent dating disaster was her fault. 'Where do I tell her my son is?'

'Don't ask me,' replied Kate. 'I'd say you're fucked.'

Minnow sighed. 'Not by Mona I won't be.'

Chapter 6

Amy and Hugh lay in bed, two spoons in the cutlery drawer of lurve. Tomorrow night they were having Daphne and Elli, Hugh's brother Gus, and another guy, Damien, over for dinner. Amy said to Hugh: 'Is it going to be fun having Damien here? I mean, he's a policeman. What if we want to have a joint? What if someone wants to drive home drunk? What if we talk about something illegal? What if we do something illegal? What will happen? Will it be uncomfortable for him? Will he feel obliged to arrest us?'

Amy turned herself belly to belly with Hugh.

'I'm just not sure that a policeman is the funnest person to have around for dinner,' she said.

'Don't worry about it, Aim. He'll be fine.'

'Yes, but what if he's not?'

'I suppose we'll all just have to apply for bail.'

'Hugh, I'm serious. It'll be weird. I'm not sure why you invited him.'

Hugh pushed Amy's hair off her face.

'Babe, Gus and I haven't seen Damien for years,' he said. 'He'll be cool. You'll like him. And besides,' he said, kissing her mouth, 'exactly what, apart from smoking drugs, would you be doing that's illegal?'

Amy smiled, and kissed Hugh back. 'I don't know,' she said, biting his lip, 'but I'm sure I could think of something.'

Friday night. Twenty-one-hundred hours. Elli looked over at Senior Constable Damien Hewitt, pulled out a spliff, and said, 'They say police have the best drugs. So tell me, how would you rate this mother?'

She passed the joint over, and Amy, Hugh, Daphne and Gus watched to see how Damien would respond. It's probably worth mentioning at this stage, that the joint Elli passed him wasn't your average, pissy little three-paper job. It was a massive spliff, constructed out of nine rollie papers. A rasta joint, very impressive. Elli had pulled it out of her handbag like some colossal, unwieldy air rifle. It had the potential to blow up in her face.

Damien looked at the joint from arm's length. He ran it under his nose with a sly smile, as if he was assessing a cigar. Or a fine wine. Or a fine woman.

'Yeah, not bad,' he said. 'I'd give it a six.'

'A six!' said Elli. 'Come on, this is good stuff.'

'Okay. Seven.'

'Seven! Fair go.'

'No, I'm afraid I can't go any higher than a seven. We get some good shit. Some of the stuff I've sampled from South America would blow you away.'

'Seven,' she said in disgust. 'Look at the workmanship. And the size. Although,' she said, pursing her lips together, 'maybe you're one of those guys who insists that size doesn't matter.'

Amy burst out laughing. She loved watching Elli flirt. It

was like watching a master at work. Elli would lean forward on her elbows, her back arched, and she'd laugh like clinking ice in a vodka and tonic. Her eyes would lock on the man of the moment, then slip coyly away, before sliding back to see if he was watching her. Her right shoulder would drop and her head would tilt to the left, displaying her long neck. Amy wondered if Elli was even aware she was doing it.

'Oh no,' Damien grinned. 'Size counts for a lot. In fact, I think size is one of the great indicators, actually.'

'Okay, so you're still telling me it's a teeny-weeny seven?' asked Elli, lifting her hand and squeezing her forefinger ever-so-close to her thumb like a little pincer.

'No. If we're talking size, I'd say it's an eye-popping nine or nine and a half out of ten.'

Elli's eyes opened wide.

'That sounds more my speed. I'd be disappointed to be sitting at the dining table with a less-than-impressive seven.'

She grinned and lit the joint, took a couple of deep drags and passed it on to Damien.

'Aren't you supposed to arrest us now or something?' Amy asked.

'Well, no, not really. I mean, if you had commercial quantities, and people were coming to your door because it was some kind of supermarket for drugs, yeah, I'd probably be concerned. But social smoking doesn't count.'

'How about social snorting?' asked Hugh, getting a foil sachet out of his pocket, as Amy collected the empty soup bowls and went into the kitchen.

'I won't, but you guys go ahead.'

'It must be a drag being a policeman,' said Elli, leaning her elbows on the table, tits smiling at Damien. 'Everyone would always be too scared to bring out their drugs, or have a good time. It'd be like being the Queen. I'll bet no one ever pulls a spliff out in front of the Queen and asks if she minds. In fact, she probably has no idea people even take drugs.'

Damien passed the joint to Daphne.

'I think she does,' said Damien. 'One of Camilla's kids was busted, wasn't he?'

'Oh yeah, that's right. Well, she probably knows people have drugs, but I'll bet she's never had any.'

'No, I reckon you're right there.'

'Actually, I feel a bit sorry for rich people,' said Elli. 'Like, say, the Queen. I'll bet she's never had a really late night at a club and gone for a souvlaki at six in the morning.'

'She might have.'

'Nuh. No way. And I'll bet she's never had a hamburger from the really good take-away shop down the road from Buckingham Palace. I'll bet she's never had baked beans on toast. Like, I can't imagine the palace kitchen bringing up her tray on a Sunday night and saying, "Sorry, I just couldn't be fagged cooking. I'm afraid it's baked beans for you tonight."'

Damien smiled at her. 'I'm sure the Queen has baked beans on toast. It's probably her most requested meal.'

'But she would never ask for it, because she would never have tasted it. She probably doesn't even know there is such a thing.'

The joint moved away from Elli's and Damien's flirting, into Daphne's and Gus's conversation pit.

'For you,' Daphne said, having a final big drag and passing the joint to Gus.

Gus smiled at her.

'Thanks.'

'So,' Daphne said, watching him coddle the joint inside

the palm of his hand and take a drag, 'you'd grow some pretty mean dope wouldn't you?'

'Why?' He glanced at her, cocking his chin in her direction. 'Because I'm a gardener?'

'Yeah.'

'You trying to get me arrested?'

'He's not even listening.'

Gus took another couple of long drags.

'Yeah, I've got a couple of plants. But I don't really smoke that much. Maybe twice a week.'

Gus examined the joint Elli had rolled.

'I used to smoke a lot, but I'm a bit over it now,' he said. 'I don't like waking up feeling hungover every morning.'

He picked a drizzle of tobacco off the tip of his tongue. Daphne had never really noticed how cute Gus was. He'd always just been Hugh's younger brother. But tonight she took a good look at him. His eyes were a sparkling, breath-of-fresh-air blue. He had a kind of a grubby look to him, not grubby-dirty, but grubby-earthy. You could tell he was a gardener. His skin was tanned. He had a few wrinkles, but they were the wrinkles from weather, not from age. Character wrinkles, instead of hello-how-are-you-I'm-at-least-forty-type wrinkles. His hair was sandy, as if he'd worked in gardens near the beach for so long that granules had actually been ingrained into his hair follicles. And his arms were strong. She'd certainly never noticed how nice his arms were. The muscles flexed and unflexed without him even noticing. When he put the joint up to his mouth, his arm unflexed, but when he put his arm back down and leant his forearm against the table, his muscle flexed. Daphne thought it should be the other way around. Shouldn't his muscle flex when he was

57

lifting his arm up, and unflex when he put it down? But it didn't. It went the other way. He looked at her sideways and smiled. She smiled back and took a deep breath. She realised that she hadn't been breathing.

'How about you?' he asked.

'Me, what?'

'Do you smoke much?'

'No. I'm probably the same as you. Once or twice a week, that's it. I get a bit bored with feeling stoned all the time too. You know, when I first moved out of home, I smoked all the time — thought it was so cool. I was at art college, and I turned up to lectures out of it the whole time. And then one day I just kind of stopped. I was sick of it.'

The joint moved on from Daphne and Gus on to Hugh. Hugh stopped what he was doing (cutting up lines of cocaine for his guests) and took the joint to Amy in the kitchen.

'Well,' Amy smiled at Hugh in a conspiratorial way, 'they all seem to be getting on rather well.'

'Yeah, I suppose so.'

Amy opened another bottle of red and poured some into her glass.

'I hate the way you do that,' she said. 'You act like you're not even noticing that they're all getting on brilliantly well. The night has the potential to be one of my most successful matchmaking ventures ever, even though admittedly you were the one who invited Damien, and I hadn't met him till tonight. But Daphne and Gus, omigod. And Elli and the Senior Sergeant Constable, if you don't mind.' Amy took a few long drags of the joint and smiled at Hugh. 'Don't you think, babe?'

She arched an eyebrow in his general direction.

'No,' he said.

Amy pouted in defiance.

'Come on. You've got to admit, it's looking damn cosy out there.'

Hugh shrugged, then wrapped Amy in his arms.

'I'll tell you what I will admit,' he said.

'What?'

'I'll admit it's looking damn cosy in here.'

Amy smiled up at him.

'And I'll also admit,' he said, 'that the soup was delicious.'

'Really?'

'Yeah. It was beautiful. You are one primo cook, baby.'

Amy passed him the joint and he picked up the bottle of red to take back into the dining room.

'How's the chicken going?' he asked as he was walking out the kitchen door.

'Nearly ready.'

'Do you want me to help?'

'No, you're right.'

Hugh went back into the dining room and passed the joint to Elli, who was seated next to him at the table.

'So, do you think I should go to the police?' Daphne was asking Damien.

Hugh sat back down and poured some red into Elli's glass. 'Go to the police about what?' he asked.

'Well, yesterday at work, this guy came in and asked if I worked there. And then when Sally said I did, he just left.'

'Why?'

'I don't know. He didn't ask to see me or anything. Sally said he was this real thuggy looking meat-head in a flannelette shirt. And then last night when I got home, you know how we've got that park opposite our flat? Well, there was a guy standing there, just watching me. But I don't know if it was the same guy or not. And I'm not even sure if he was watching me, or just standing, not watching me, but facing in my direction. Do you know what I mean?'

Hugh resumed the coke cutting.

'Yeah. So who is he?'

'Well, I don't know,' said Daphne.

'Have you seen him, Elli?' Damien asked.

'No. But I don't get home until late on a Thursday night.'

'What about today? Was he there this morning?' Gus asked.

'No. I didn't see him. But then, today, my creative direc-tor came in and said some guy had been on the phone, asking what accounts I work on.'

Hugh neatly divvied up the coke, pulled out a ten-dollar note from his pocket, rolled it up, and snorted a line. He looked over at Daphne.

'Same guy?' he asked.

'Well, I assume so.'

Gus took the rolled-up bill from Hugh and snorted a line. He sniffed, and wiped his nose with the back of his hand.

'Have you got one of those screamer alarm things?' Gus asked Daphne.

'No,' she said.

'You should get one,' he said.

He passed her the rolled-up ten-dollar bill.

'Thanks,' Daphne said.

She leant across Gus to where the cocaine was. Gus didn't move out of her way, and he didn't put the cocaine any closer to her. He stayed where he was, and the cocaine stayed where it was, so Daphne had to touch his chest with her arm.

'I hate that some creep is following you,' he said, as she came up for air like some kind of scuba-diving dinner-party guest, her snorkel a ten-dollar note.

She smiled at him. 'Look, it's probably nothing. It's just a
bit weird. I wasn't too freaked, until Lizzie told me about the
phone call today.' Daphne passed the coke straw and the tray
with the cocaine on it to Elli. She turned back to Gus, who
handed her the joint. She took a drag.

'Do you like Cactus?' he asked.

'Yeah. I only know a couple of their songs, but I like what
I've heard so far,' she said.

'They're playing next Friday night at The Espy. I'm going
with some friends. Do you want to come?'

She smiled at him. 'Yeah, that'd be good.'

She took another drag of the joint.

Amy came out of the kitchen holding three plates of
chicken and looked at her guests. The ten-dollar bill was now
up Elli's nose.

'Good one, Hugh,' Amy said. 'No one's gonna want to eat
now.'

Hugh looked up at Amy and sniffed. He winked at her.

'Sure they will, Aim. Actually, I gave them the coke for
medicinal purposes, to counteract the sedative effects caused
by the wine and the dope. This way, they won't fall asleep at
the table. I only did it for you, baby,' he said. 'I thought you'd
appreciate it.'

'Yeah right,' said Amy, putting the plates in front of Elli,
Daphne and Damien.

'If you have dope, and then you have cocaine, does the
cocaine cancel out the munchies you usually get with dope?'
Elli asked. Then she looked up guiltily at Amy and said, 'But
I'm still really hungry, even though I've had a line. And this
looks fantastic.'

Amy clicked her tongue and went back into the kitchen.
She came out with hers, Hugh's and Gus's plates.

There was a lull as everyone cut meat and started eating, followed by the overenthusiasm that drugs can sometimes induce.

'This is really fantastic, Amy.'

'Stupendiddlyumptious.'

'Wondiddlyunderful.'

'Yeah, enough already,' said Amy, rolling her eyes.

Chicken, cocaine, dope, and wine. A fine meal by any standards. The conversation fired up, spiralling in chaotic, unrelated circles, everyone following it like little doped-up lambs. Gus, Hugh, Daphne and Amy in one conversation.

'Children are like pancakes,' said Gus, rolling another joint. 'The first one never comes out right.'

'Fuck off,' said Hugh, passing Gus a filter he'd made for the joint.

Elli and Damien were having their own conversation.

'If I had to join the army, like, say we had conscription, I'd prefer to live in Switzerland,' said Elli.

'Why, because they don't have conscription?'

'No, because if I had to join an army, the Swiss Army would be the most fun. Say, for example,' she continued, cutting her chicken, 'their knife. It has a bottle opener, a nail-file and a pair of scissors. No bayonets or anything yukky. Just nice, civilised things. I imagine they all just sit around the fire at night, doing their nails, drinking chardonnay, hair in rollers, having a lovely time.'

And back down the other end of the table, 'I'd have thought you'd come up with a gardening metaphor, not a cooking one,' said Daphne.

'I'm good in the kitchen too, you know,' said Gus.

'And I'll bet they have really nice uniforms. The same shade as their nail polish. And they'd just sit around Checkpoint

Charlie, polishing their shoes, and fixing their hair, looking fabulous in the event of an enemy invasion.'

'What other rooms are you good in?' Daphne asked Gus.

'Omigod. Do you mind?' asked Amy, sticking her fingers down her throat as if she was needing to vomit.

'What?' Daphne asked, opening her eyes as innocently wide as they'd go.

'What other rooms are you good in?' mimicked Amy.

Gus laughed. 'Piss off, Amy.'

Daphne grinned naughtily.

'Elli and I watched that Demi Moore movie on Tuesday night,' said Daphne, changing the subject before it got too obvious that she was flirting wildly with Gus. 'You know, the one where she sleeps with Robert Redford for a million dollars.'

'I remember that. What was it called again?' asked Amy.

'*Indecent Proposal.* God, it was a bad film.'

'It was terrible,' agreed Elli, slipping into their conversation. She didn't want it to be too obvious that she and Damien were doing some pretty hardcore flirting themselves, down the other end of the table. 'She was so annoying, and he was so ugly. As if she'd have slept with him.'

'Yeah right, Elli,' said Hugh. 'You're saying you wouldn't sleep with Robert Redford for a million dollars?'

'No. No way. He's foul. His skin's all pock-marked.'

'He was a spunk when he was younger, but yeah, he's certainly no babe now,' said Amy.

Hugh looked at Amy. 'You wouldn't sleep with him either? For a million dollars?'

'No. Why? Would you make me?'

'Yeah, for sure. You could buy me a new board.'

'Get lost. There's no way.'

'I would,' said Daphne. 'I think he's still really handsome.'

'Couldn't think of anything worse,' said Elli. She looked at Damien. Time to get back to their own personal conversation, she figured, adjusting her boobs.

'I would too,' said Damien.

The table looked at him. Elli flushed.

'You would?' she asked.

'Shit yeah. For a million bucks. Sure I would. In fact,' he added, 'I'd have to say I'd sleep with Robert Redford for a lot less than a million dollars.'

Daphne looked at Elli. Elli looked at Damien.

'Fuck,' she said the next morning to Daphne, 'what is wrong with me? I spend half my time thinking about Ben, and the other half flirting with some fucking nancy boy.'

She took a swig of her orange juice and cheers'd Daphne.

'I'm not bad at this single-girl shit, am I? God. Anyway, tell me about you and Gus.'

Chapter 7

Kate had been right. The picnic with Mona? He'd been fucked. Missionary style, doggy style, up against the wall, on the kitchen bench.

'I'm dying to meet your little boy,' Mona had said at the end of round four.

Lochie came into the lounge room, Monopoly under his arm, and jumped onto Minnow's lap.

'No way,' said Kate. 'No Monopoly, it takes too long. I want him to have an early night. He was in such a grump this morning,' she said to Minnow.

'You're to be in bed by eight,' she told Lochie.

'Eight!' said Lochie. 'That's not fair. It's Friday night.'

'Bad luck. You've got Auskick tomorrow morning. Early. So, bed by eight.'

'But Mum, we always play Monopoly. Whenever he babysits.'

'Not always. Not tonight, for example.'

'Oh God!' said Lochie, fists clenched around the Monopoly board as he climbed off Minnow's lap and stomped to his bedroom.

'That's okay,' said Minnow. 'Doug's coming over, and we're going to watch the footy anyway. I'll make sure he's in bed by eight.'

'Thanks.'

'So where's Cactus playing tonight?' Minnow asked.

'The Espy,' Kate said.

'Who's supporting?' he asked.

'I'm not sure,' said Kate. 'Do you know?' she asked Ben.

'Pure Honey. They're not bad.'

'Right,' said Minnow. 'That should be good. Cactus are excellent.'

'Yeah. We supported them a couple of weeks ago,' said Ben. 'Their bass player is awesome.'

'He used to play with Kate Ceberano, didn't he?'

'Yeah.'

'So what time are they coming on? Eleven?'

'I'd say so,' said Ben.

'We're going to grab something to eat first,' said Kate, 'but I've got my mobile if you need me.'

'Okay. Well, have a good time,' said Minnow.

'Bye, Loch,' called Kate. No reply. She looked at Minnow and pursed her mouth in sympathy.

'Sorry to leave you with such a bad-tempered child,' she said.

'Don't sweat it,' he said. 'He'll be fine.'

Minnow closed the door behind Kate and Ben. He went into Lochie's bedroom. Lochie was sitting on his bed sullenly. Minnow cupped the sad little chin in his hand and tilted Lochie's face up towards him.

'Hey, why so glum?'

'I wanted to play Monopoly.'

Minnow smiled at Lochie. 'Well, of course we're going to play Monopoly. You didn't believe me when I said you were going to bed at eight? No way, man, I just said that to get your mum off your case. We are playing the game. Pick it up. Doug'll be over in a minute. Tonight,' he said, linking his fingers and turning his hands inside out, away from his body, a click coming from his knuckles, 'I'm going to whip both your arses.'

Lochie looked up at Minnow, eyes wide. 'Really?'

'Definitely. That's the only reason I agree to babysit you. To beat you at Monopoly.'

'Fat chance,' said Lochie, picking up the challenge together with the Monopoly board, and heading for the lounge room.

'I want to be the car,' Lochie said, as he took the board and all the pieces out of the box.

'Bad luck,' said Minnow. 'I'm the car. You can be the ship.'

'But you're always the car.'

'Exactly.'

Lochie set the board up on the table. Minnow started divvying up the money, and colour coding the properties.

'You can be the banker,' he told Lochie, handing over wads of cash.

'Thanks.'

'And I'm the real estate agent.'

'Alright.'

There was a knock at the door.

'Go get it,' Minnow said. 'That'll be Doug.'

'Iqbal,' Minnow could hear Doug say as he was led into

the lounge by Lochie. 'Eight o'clock. That was never gonna happen. Your mum, eh. We love her but seriously, she's got no idea, has she? Bags the car.'

'Mine,' said Minnow.

'Okay. I'll be the ship.'

Lochie grinned. 'That's me.'

Doug raised his lip in distaste. 'Don't tell me, I'm the dog again?'

Lochie barked as he showed Doug what was in his hand. 'Woof.'

Doug grabbed Lochie, hard, in a headlock and started belting the bejesus out of him. Lochie screamed and punched his way out of Doug's grip. Minnow grabbed Lochie, and held both arms back so that his little stomach was exposed to Doug's man-sized fists. Doug started pummelling. Lochie, not prepared to give up the good fight, started kicking Doug. Minnow and Doug wrestled him onto the floor. Doug sat on his legs, pinned his arms to the ground with his knees and started typing on his chest.

'Give up?'

'No,' said Lochie, writhing and giggling.

'Are you going to let me be the ship?'

'Never.'

'Give me the ship.'

'No.' Lochie struggled, as he Houdini-ed his way out from under Doug and raced into his bedroom.

Doug took two heavy, lumbering, threatening steps in Lochie's direction, then sat down on the couch. Minnow passed him a beer from the stash.

Lochie came out, holding the dog. 'Do you want it?' He whistled to Doug. 'Here boy.'

Doug jumped up, Lochie dived for his bedroom. Doug sat back down again.

'So,' said Doug, 'how's it going with Mona?'

Minnow shrugged. 'Yeah, she's okay.'

Lochie came back out of his room, teasing Doug with the dog. Doug waited until Lochie was within grabbing distance, then shot an arm out and wrapped it around Lochie's torso. He pulled Lochie down on the couch, boxed him around the ears, took the dog, and set it down on the board. He handed the dice to Lochie.

'You start,' he said.

Minnow passed Lochie a Coke from the stash.

'Go grab us a bowl, mate,' he said to Lochie.

Lochie went into the kitchen and got a bowl. Minnow tipped the box of Cheezels in. Lochie put a Cheezel on each finger and rolled the dice.

'Angel Islington. I'll buy,' said Lochie.

'You don't want to buy that. It's crap,' said Minnow.

'I like it. I'm buying it.'

'I've told you before. Never buy the blue ones.'

'Give it here.'

'It's a bad buy.'

'I don't care.'

Minnow shook his head and passed Lochie the 'crappest property on the board. No question'.

At 8.30 the television went on. Collingwood versus Essendon. A classic clash. Minnow and Doug became increasingly distracted by the game and decreasingly interested in Monopoly. Eventually, Lochie asked: 'Are you guys still playing?'

'Yeah. 'Course.'

'Course they weren't. Ten minutes later, Lochie also abandoned Monopoly and sat on Minnow's knee to watch the game. At half-time Minnow pushed Lochie off his knee. 'Okay. Toilet, teeth, bed.'

'No, not yet.'

'Yes, now. You were supposed to be in bed at eight o'clock, remember? It's now nearly ten.'

'Is it?' Lochie sounded pleased.

'Yes. Your mum'd have a fit if she knew you were still up. So go brush your teeth and call me when you've finished. I'll read you a quick story.'

'Okay,' and Lochie went quietly off to stand in the doorway, watching the telly, not going into the bathroom at all. Minnow looked over.

'Mate,' he said.

'Yeah, okay,' and Lochie wandered off to the bathroom. He came back in and gave Doug a kiss good night.

'See you next time, matey,' said Doug.

'Okay. Thanks for the game.'

'Yeah, it was good.'

'Are you ready?' Lochie asked Minnow.

'Yep. Come on.' Minnow stood up and Lochie led him into the bedroom.

Doug listened quietly. He could hear Lochie and Minnow arguing. Minnow was saying 'No, that's too long. A quick book, I said. No, not that one either. Here, I'll choose. This one.'

'No, not that one. This one.'

'Alright, but as soon as the second half starts, I'm stopping. I don't care if we've finished it or not.'

'Okay.'

And Minnow started reading. Doug got up and went into the kitchen. He picked up the phone. He dialled 9532 6969.

'Hello?'

'Hi Jacinta,' he said quietly. 'It's me.'

'Minnow?'

'Yeah. How are you going?'

'I'm good. How are you?'

'Yeah, good. What are you doing tonight?'

'Nothing. I'm just at home. What are you doing?'

'I'm over at a mate's place, watching the footy. But I thought I might drop around later.'

'Yeah, that'd be great.'

'Okay. I've gotta go. The third quarter's about to start.'

'Okay. I'll see you when you get here. Hey, Minnow.'

'Yeah.'

'I'm looking forward to seeing you again.'

'Me too. I'll see you in a little while. Bye.'

And Doug hung up the phone. He called out to Minnow. 'Do you want another beer?'

'Yeah, thanks,' Minnow called back.

Doug grabbed two beers from the fridge and went back into the lounge room. He sat in front of the telly, not watching. Thinking. Thinking of Jacinta.

He hadn't expected to like her much. Three weeks it had been. Three weeks since he'd rung her that afternoon at Crush when he was with Kate and Minnow. Three weeks since he'd knocked on a door he didn't know, which was opened by a girl he didn't recognise. She was tall and slim, an angel's face, with soft, straight, long blonde hair. Cut to, well, cut to nipple height actually. Doug had wondered how she briefed her hairdresser.

'Just to my nipples, thanks.'

'Sure. Layers the same?'

'Yep.'

Then he had moved Jacinta away from the hairdresser, back to her apartment, standing here in front of him, and thought, 'Is she going to pick up that I'm not Minnow, or was she really that drunk?'

She had these gigantic, sexy-as lips which she anchored to Doug's mouth as soon as he stepped inside her flat. It seemed she hadn't picked up that he wasn't really Minnow.

She stepped back from the pash.

'Hi.'

She smiled.

'Hi,' said Doug, smiling.

And then Jacinta moved back in towards him. Doug had moved his hands over her body, put his arms around her torso, moved his hands down her back. Spread his fingers to capture every inch of her tiny butt. Held his hand firm and pulled her body closer to his. Jacinta stepped backwards, away from the front door, keeping her lips locked on his.

She shimmied into the first door off the hallway. Doug followed, keenly aware that behind her was a bed. She shed her snakeskin coat. Doug lifted her tight black top up over her languid arms. Her bra was a gentle lilac, with flowers delicately embroidered over it. Doug barely noticed it, unhooked it, peeled it from her, and dumped it on the floor. He started unbuttoning her pants.

'Have you booked the table for any particular time, Minnow?' she'd asked, and suddenly, just for a moment, not long at all, hardly any time really, just when she called him Minnow, he felt a softening. Not much of a softening, certainly she wouldn't have noticed it, it was still rock-hard all things considered, but he felt a surge of guilt. Then he felt another surge, and the question of guilt left his mind altogether.

'How was it?' Minnow had asked the next day.

'Great sex,' said Doug.

And that was where he left it. For about two days. A night of good sex. A one-night stand. A fuck is a fuck, not a relationship.

But about two days later he found himself thinking, over and over, 9532 6969. Driving to work. 9532 6969. Having a shower. 9532 6969. Having a beer with Minnow. 9532 6969. He'd gone home that night and called her. He hadn't intended to; it had taken him completely by surprise when he found himself on the phone chatting to her, organising to catch up again the next night. And the next night it had been the same. She'd opened the door, her beautiful angel face tilted up at him, her gigantic, sexy-as lips anchored to his mouth as soon as he stepped inside her flat. Her top off, before he could even register what she was wearing.

He didn't tell Minnow. Minnow wasn't his mother. He didn't have to tell Minnow everything he did, every time he had sex. He wasn't a kid, needing his mate's thumbs-up whenever he scored. He didn't tell Minnow everything, and he was pretty sure Minnow didn't tell him everything. They were mates, not Catholic schoolboys, having to confess every little thing they did. And the third time he'd gone around to Jacinta's place, he hadn't mentioned it to anyone. Or the fourth time. Or the fifth time. And now the opportunity to mention it had gone. Jacinta had been weeks ago, as far as Minnow and Kate were concerned. If he mentioned her now, it would be weird. So the moment had gone. Long gone. It's a funny thing, but there's a certain, unspecified time frame in which to bring something up. But if you pass that window of opportunity and don't climb through it, it suddenly slams shut. And to talk about it after that time requires some pretty heavy-handed jemmying, and everyone feels vaguely violated because the timing is now all wrong.

He'd mention her in a couple of weeks to those guys. Say he'd seen her out one night and gone back to her place. That he might call her again. That he quite liked her. That he dug her in a big way. He'd mention it to them in a week or two. He'd explain to them that Jacinta wasn't at all how Minnow had described her. She wasn't pushy or desperate. She was interesting. She was funny. She was sweet. Admittedly, she was no brain surgeon, but then again, his brain didn't need an operation. She liked the same movies he did. She cooked really nice meals. She had applied to study interior design but didn't know if she was in yet. There were all these things about her that Minnow hadn't told them, that Minnow didn't know. Once Minnow and Kate got to know her as Doug's girlfriend, they'd really like her. For sure they would.

There was only one other problem. He'd neglected to mention to Jacinta his real name. Jacinta was still calling him Minnow, and he hadn't worked out the most appropriate way to tell her that his name was Doug. He'd work it out. He'd tell her. He'd get on to it. Soon enough. Absolutely. Definitely. He just had to figure out how to break it to her. How to bring it up, without necessarily telling her about her first night with Minnow. Because he was pretty sure that she wouldn't see the funny side of him taking her out as Min-now. But in the end it was all semantics. Details. Small stuff. And he wasn't interested in the fine print. He was interested in the bigger picture. He'd get down to minor details like what his real name was, later.

Chapter 8

Daphne sat on the couch. 7:48 p.m. She went into the bathroom to check her lippie, then went back into the lounge room and sat down again. 7:49 p.m. She got back up and went into the bathroom. How was her hair? Did it look like she'd gone to too much effort? Was there too much wax in it? Were the flowers wrong? Did they look pretty? Or pretentious? She turned away from the mirror, then turned quickly back, imagining she was catching sight of herself for the first time. No, her hair was fine. What about the boots? Did they look cool, or come-fuck-me? If she was wearing a shorter skirt they would probably look a bit come-fuck-me, but with what she was wearing they looked good. One inch of skin between skirt and boot. Black top, tight. Yeah, that looked bonus. She went back and sat on the couch. 7:54 p.m. She got up and went back into the bathroom. Was her lippie too obvious? Red. She didn't normally wear red. She was more of a brown girl herself. Red was more Elli. It would be good if Elli was here. If Elli was here, Daphne wouldn't be spending all this time at the bathroom mirror, honing in on every flaw with military precision. If Elli was here, they'd be sitting on the couch quaffing some wine, instead of Daphne sitting, standing, sitting, standing, waiting, waiting, waiting, for Gus to collect her.

Collect her. That was the weird thing about dating. Daphne considered herself to be a woman of the moment. Independent. Wise beyond her years. Alright, the part about being wise beyond her years was bullshit, but the independent part was right. Yet here she was, waiting for Gus to 'collect' her. Like his dry-cleaning.

Daphne wiped off the red. Best to stick with what you know works. A slash of brown. Much better. She went back into the lounge room and sat down. She got back up and went into the kitchen for a glass of water. Then she went into the bathroom for a change. She pressed the inside of her wrist against her nose and breathed in. Should she put on more perfume? She could hardly smell it, but maybe that was because she was used to it. If she put on more, it might be too much. She decided against a direct application, but hedged her bets by spraying a shot of perfume in the air and walking through it. It was something her mum used to do. 'A random application according to the chaos theory of perfume,' her mum would say. Her mum was scary sometimes.

Daphne went back into the lounge room. Some music, that's what was needed. She knelt down and flicked through her collection. Underground Lovers? Too mellow, too schmoozy. Mazzy Star? Maybe. The Charlatans? A possibility, although probably not right for the sitting-at-home-waiting-for-your-date-to-'collect'-you-scenario. Billy Bragg? A good balance between '70s Bob Dylan and your fired-up-rock-star-approach. Ben Harper? Yeah, Ben could be the thing. Might do the job. Daphne read the back of the CD. Actually, Ben was probably a good choice. Mellow, soulful, but also a bit of edge.

Daphne thought he was definitely a contender. The frontrunner in fact. Daphne rubbed her eye, flicked through a couple more CDs just to be fair, then settled on Ben.

She went back into the bathroom to check that she hadn't smeared mascara all over her eye when she'd rubbed it. She had a bit. She wiped it off, put on more. Went back into the lounge room. Sat down. Listened to Ben. Heard a car. Got up and went to the window to see if it was Gus. It wasn't. She looked into the park opposite to see if that guy was there again. He wasn't. She sat back down.

She stood back up and went over to the bookcase. Pulled out an old photo album and opened it. There was her, Amy, and Elli, first year at art school. God, look at those earrings. I mean sure, hoops are fine, but they weren't hoops she was wearing. They were hula hoops. A few pages on was a photo of her, 'The Bastard', Amy, and Hugh, on the beach in Bali. It was night, there was a bottle of vodka between them. Her arm was slung around 'The Bastard's' shoulder, pulling him in towards her. She was laughing. Amy and Hugh were leaning in towards them, making sure they were all in frame.

It was more than a year since she'd broken up with 'The Bastard', and she still had such a sour taste in her mouth over all the shit that had gone down. It made her feel sad to see this photo, to see how much she had liked him, the way she wanted him right next to her, right there, close to her. She shut the album and went back into the bathroom. Yep, she still looked the same as she had five minutes ago. She went into the kitchen and looked in the pantry, knowing that she wouldn't eat anything because she'd just brushed her teeth.

And then there was a knock on the door. She gripped her stomach, went back into the bathroom for a quick spot-check, then answered the door.

'Hi,' she said, smiling.

'Hi,' he said, smiling back.

Should she lean in and give him a kiss hello? What was appropriate? Would it be too forward if she did? Would it be too unfriendly if she didn't? She decided against it, and stepped back for him to come inside. He was taller than she'd realised. She'd always thought of him as Hugh's little brother, but now, as he stepped past her into the lounge room, she forgot his association with Hugh and just saw him as a tall, muscly, manly man, who made her feel all small and light and girly in comparison. She noticed that he smelt nice — earthy. And looked exceptionally good. He was wearing a plain khaki jumper, with a white T-shirt underneath, and sandy coloured pants.

'You like Ben?' he asked, nodding towards the CD player.

'Yeah, I do,' said Daphne. 'How about you?'

'Yeah, he's awesome. Last year I was in Byron with some friends, and he played at the festival up there.'

'That would have been fantastic.'

'Yeah, he was brilliant.'

Gus squatted down and started looking through her CDs. She heard a small click from his knees.

'This is good,' he said, holding up Billy Bragg.

'I love that.'

'And this is good too.'

'Yeah.'

Daphne watched his back as he leant over the CD cabinet. He was broad, but not too big — a gentle, strong back. For a moment she forgot that she didn't know him that well, and nearly went over to him, slid her hands through the handles his arms made, through to his stomach. She folded her arms in front to keep them under her stern control. Chitchat.

Small talk. 'Do you want a drink?' That type of thing. He told her he'd arranged to meet his friends at The Espy around ten to see Cactus, but he thought the two of them might grab something to eat at The Kitchen beforehand.

He drove an old Valiant. Beige. Rusted. A monster. Gold fringing dangled from the roof near the windscreen, secured at either end by the sun visors. She ran her fingers through the fringing. It gave the grungy car a butt-slap of glamour.

'The girl I bought the car off put it there,' he said. 'I never took it off. I quite like it.'

The Espy was packed. They walked past the pool tables, out through the back to The Kitchen. Daphne loved the burgers they had there, but decided that wrapping her mouth around a burger on a first date was not the way to play it, so she ordered a stir-fry instead. Gus went to order, and Daphne watched his back, watching him chat to the guy behind the counter. The guy behind the counter leaned forward on his elbows and said something to Gus, looked over at Daphne, and smiled. Daphne smiled back. Gus walked back to the table. Daphne was about to ask Gus what the guy had said, but just as Gus sat down, someone put their hand on Daphne's shoulder. She turned around and looked up.

Ben. Elli's old Ben. Daphne felt a smile bubble to her mouth.

'Hi,' she said.

'Hi,' he said, grinning at her. 'How's it going?'

'Omigod,' Elli said the next morning. 'How was he? How did he look? Is he still seeing Kate? Did you meet her? What's she like? Did they look happy? Is she pretty? What was she wearing? Was she nice? Did you talk to her? Did she know you were a friend of mine?' And then finally, she asked, 'Anyway, what happened with you and Gus?'

Gus and Daphne walked back to the car, which was parked outside Luna Park. The scenic railway line heaved its way silently through the darkness of St Kilda. They chatted in the car as he drove her home, same as before, but there was something new in the car between them. An anticipation. An uncertainty. A kiss. Or maybe not.

He parked in front of her flats, turned his car off, but left his seat belt on. Was that a signal that he wasn't staying long? Daphne smiled at him.

'Thanks for tonight,' she said. 'It was fun. Your friends are really nice. I had a great time.'

'Me too.'

She turned away from him to open her door.

'Hey, have you seen that guy again?' Gus asked. 'You know, the one who was following you last week?'

Daphne turned back to face him.

'No. Oh, actually, there was one morning when I thought I saw him, but then I don't think I did. I think I was just imagining it.'

'If you see him again, you should call the police. Straight-away.'

'Do you think?' asked Daphne. 'But he's probably not following me. It's probably just a coincidence.'

She looked down at her hands. Gus made no move to kiss her. She looked up at him and smiled.

'Anyway, thanks again for tonight,' she said.

'Yeah, thanks for coming with me. I s'pose I'll see you round.'

'Yeah, okay.'

A disappointed feeling spread through Daphne's arms, making them feel heavy. She leant over and gave Gus a kiss on the cheek. He picked up her hand and kissed the tips of her fingers. Then he put his hand behind her head and pulled her towards him. He kissed her mouth. She felt his tongue gently opening her mouth, his body entering her space. He undid his seat belt and put his arms around her. They pulled apart, looked at each other shyly, then moved back in to kiss some more. Delicious.

After a while, she murmured, 'Would you like to come up?'

'I'd love to. But I'd better not. I'm working tomorrow, and I've got to be up early.'

'Okay.'

'What are you doing next week?' he asked.

'Um, just working.'

'Would you like to go out one night?'

She smiled. 'Yeah, I'd love to.'

'Okay, I'll give you a call.'

'That'd be good.' Daphne got out of his car and went inside. She felt giggly. Bubbles in her legs gave her the over-whelming desire to jump up and down. She wanted to wake up Elli. She certainly couldn't sleep. She went into the bath-room but decided against washing off her makeup. She didn't want to brush her teeth, either. She didn't want to wash any of Gus off. She could taste him in her mouth. Smell him on her clothes. In her hair. She turned on the telly. Cactus's new song was on.

'That's an omen for sure,' said Elli.

She sat at the breakfast bench the next morning as

Daphne detailed the night before. Daphne's hair was messy, with pins and fallen flowers, from where she'd slept on it. Mascara was crawling underneath her lashes, and she was wearing her best, just-in-case-we-have-sex knickers, a singlet, and cosy, lambskin boots.

'Do you think so?' asked Daphne. 'I mean, it's probably not, it's probably just a coincidence, but it felt like an omen. Like, to turn on the telly and for Cactus to be singing just at that moment.'

'That's definitely spooky. I'm sure it means something.'

Daphne grinned and filled the kettle with water.

'Do you want a cup of tea?'

'No, not just yet,' said Elli. 'I'm going to have a shower.'

Elli left the kitchen and walked down the corridor. She shut the door of the bathroom and looked at herself in the mirror.

'Fuck.' So Ben had been at The Espy last night with Kate. She wished Daphne hadn't told her, but in a way she had liked hearing it. It was almost like wobbling a loose tooth when you were in primary school. It hurt, but it was kind of satisfying at the same time. She had thought about Kate so many times, wondered what she was like, what Ben saw in her, what she looked like, whether she looked mumsy or not. She thought about how she might have seen Kate on the street or at a bar, but not known it was her. Daphne said she was tall. Straight, dark hair, in plaits. A bit Asian-looking. Wearing jeans and a Norton singlet, with a jumper tied around her waist. Daphne said she wasn't really all that attractive, 'not half as pretty as you' she'd said, but she hadn't sounded terribly convincing. Elli suspected Daphne was just trying to spare her feelings. Fucking Ben. She hadn't seen

Ben for months. The last time she'd seen him was the night he'd come into Franco's, when Elli was still working there, and told her he was seeing someone else now. A girl called Kate. A single mum. Her kid was about eight, he'd said.

'You'd like her,' he'd said.

Elli got her gear off, T-shirt over the head, undies flicked down her legs. She studied her reflection in the bathroom mirror. The body is hardly an erotic proposition when it's just standing there, waiting to perform necessary ablutions. It's very utilitarian when you look at it objectively. Walks. Bends over. Gets into shower. Moves soap over body to wash skin. Lifts arms up in order to wash hair. Functional, pedestrian, hardly a thing of inspiration. Elli added more hot water to the mix and watched the lather from the shampoo pool at her feet before it scooted down the drain.

Everyone but Elli, it seemed, was able to get a relationship happening. Ben and Kate. Daphne and Gus. The only relationships Elli had had recently was for about two hours last week with a policeman who got a schwing over Robert Redford, and that guy Minnow, from a month ago, but you'd hardly call either of those a 'relationship'.

Elli got out of the shower and dried herself roughly, trying to rub away the bad thoughts which were scattered like dandruff over her head and shoulders. She couldn't stand the way she still ached for Ben. It was a physical ache. A bruise that just wouldn't go away. She felt like the personification of 'lacklustre'. No wonder Damien would rather sleep with Robert Redford than her. She started blow-drying her hair and wondered what it was like to suffer from real depression. Serious, medication-dependent depression. To every morning wake up and mercilessly pick on yourself, refusing to see anything good in the mirror, to walk around the house dragging your lethargic, heavy shadow after you, to wish you were with anybody, anywhere, but here, with your own self.

She walked into her bedroom and opened her wardrobe door. Of course, not a single item dangled enticingly from her coat hangers. It all just hung there, limply. Red. She needed something red. Desperate times called for desperate measures. She got out her red Morrisey top. And her green Scanlan & Theodore pants. And her Chinese beaded slippers. And some purple hairpins. And even just laying them on her bed made her feel better. She set to work. She put her clothes on. She pushed her hair up. Up. All her hair up, up, up. Lots of purple hairpins.

And suddenly, she felt better. Sure, she didn't feel kick-arse, but she certainly felt a whole heap more primo than she had when it had just been her and her naked body, alone in the bathroom. Lipstick. Eyeliner. Mascara. Yeah, things weren't so bad. Life was okay. Ben could go fuck himself. Damien could go fuck Robert Redford. She'd go and buy something. She walked into the kitchen.

'Daph, do you feel like going shopping?'

'Always.'

Elli walked back into her bedroom to grab her bag. Things were looking up. So what if everyone else was having sex and she was having zip.

'Boys are like trams,' she said to herself. 'There'll be another one along any minute.'

Chapter 9

The customer on table three had finally left the restaurant. Elli cleared his table, unfolding a piece of paper he'd left in the bill folder, as she walked back to the bar.

'Have a look at this,' she said to Tristan.

Tristan opened the paper. Inside was a drawing of a penis, with an arrow pointing to the head of it. 'Here's your tip' was written in capital letters.

'That's nice,' he said.

'Lovely,' she agreed, picking up two pots of tea for table four. 'Hopefully he'll become a regular, and I'll get to serve him all the time.'

'Fingers crossed.'

Tristan's day so far: worked a double, even though he was supposed to have had tonight off. Philby had dropped one of the platters, which was worth a fucking shitload of money. Jacinta had pissed off early. Elli had freaked out because she thought some guy was following her, and started raving on about how she thought it was the same one who'd followed Daphne, her flatmate, last week. And table three had been a complete cunt. The only good thing about the day was that it was nearly over.

You'd think a place called The Tea House would be ordered and serene, run by meek, mild geisha girls tottering around in kimonos, black hair in buns, bowing left and right, giggling coyly behind their hands, subservient to the end. No, it wasn't like that at all. The whole place was very minimal, nothing on the white walls at all except for one small Tetley tea bag framed by an enormous, over-sized border, a delicate joke positioned in the centre of the left wall. A simple wooden counter ran the length of the right wall, with glass shelves holding canisters of about a gazillion different herbal teas. Tea was brought out to customers on a laquered black tray, in a hold-it-too-tight-and-you'll-crush-it-with-your-bare-hands china teapot of a startlingly bright colour. Cobalt. Citrus. Fire. Emerald. Fuschia. The teacups were of the same eggshell-fine china, in a jolting colour contrast to the teapot. Meals were served on square, paper-thin plates which, if held up to the light, bounced rainbow hues onto the floor. The girls wore tight white singlets with white, wide leg pants, and beaded slippers. The boys wore black singlets, with black pants, and Birkenstocks. There was no coy giggling behind hands. The menu currently read like this:

Ambrosia of oysters on a chilled clambake of cucumber.

Beanfeast of vegetables sozzled in consomme.

Tuna tataki with a collaboration of Asian sauces.

Succotash of swordfish with holus bolus of vegetables and wilted beetroot leaves.

You get the general idea. Every month Dave and Tristan would open a couple of bottles of wine, cut up some cocaine, and run the staff through the new menu. They'd all sit around the thesaurus picking out the most ridiculous descriptions they could think of — the succotash of swordfish was one of Tristan's, of which he was particularly proud.

Elli came up to the bar and pinched Tristan.

'Ow.'

'See that guy who's just walked in?' she said.

'Shit. I was wanting to finish up soon. Tell him the kitchen's closed. They can have dessert if they're hungry.'

'I can't. Remember a few weeks ago at The Martini Den? About a month ago? That guy I kissed? Minnow? That's him. Philby'll have to serve them, I'm too embarrassed.'

'Don't be ridiculous.'

Elli shook her head. 'No. Can't. Serious.'

'Elli.'

'Definitely not.'

Tristan sighed. 'Okay. I'll put them on table nine.'

'Thanks, you're a pal,' said Elli.

Philby was briefed on the situation.

'I need to know who the girl is, what they're talking about, and, especially, if he's noticed me.'

'Yeah, yeah, whatever,' said Philby as he ambled over to their table.

'Two glasses of the Evans & Tate. They've just seen a movie,' he said, when he returned from taking their order.

'Which one?'

'Not sure.'

Elli poured the wine into two delicate glasses and put them on a laquered tray. She leaned her elbows on the bar and watched Philby place the glasses in front of them.

'I'm sorry,' she said, 'but since when have clips been in? Pins, yes. Clips, no.'

'What?' said Tristan.

'Those clips that the girl he's with has got in her hair.

They're so not-cool.' Tristan smiled at Elli and slid some freshly polished glasses into the corrals above the bar. The glasses hung, suspended like overblown crystal bats.

'And that jumper,' she said. 'You can't tell me that looks good.'

He glanced over at table nine.

'It's alright.'

'Oh, come on. You can't be serious? The skirt's okay, but the jumper and the clips are awful. They really let her down.'

Philby came back to the wooden counter with their dessert orders.

'Apple tart to share. And her name's Mona.'

'Mona. What kind of a name is that?'

Elli went into the kitchen.

'Tart for the tart on table nine,' she said.

A short time later.

'Two more Evans & Tate, and they work together.'

'That's interesting,' Elli said, as she poured two more glasses, 'because I remember he wasn't working the night I met him. Although, I think he said he had a job interview coming up later that week. So, he must have gotten the job.'

Elli heard the bell and went into the kitchen. She came back out and put the apple tart on the counter for Philby to take over.

'Crystallised violetine of apple brioche for table nine,' she said.

Philby took it over. He came back to the counter.

'It must be a new relationship, because she hasn't seen his place yet.'

'Right.' Elli cleared table three, and connected with Philby on the way back to the bar.

'Two camellia teas and general chitchat,' he said.

Elli went back behind the bar and 'romanced' an aurora borealis-pink teapot with boiling water, before tipping the water out, and putting two spoons of fragrant tea leaves in, and more boiling water. She placed the pot on the lacquered tray with two incandescent orange cups, and a delicate tea strainer. Philby took the tray over and poured their teas. He came back to the bar.

'She's asking him about his ex.'

'Ooh, that's interesting. What's he saying?'

'Why do girls always want to ask the one question guys don't want to talk about?'

'Why do guys not want to talk about the one thing that's really interesting?'

Philby went to see how they were going with their tea. He came back to the bar.

'The bill, please. She's asking when she can meet his little boy.'

'What do you mean?'

'Well, she says she wants to meet him.'

'Who?'

'His little boy.'

'What little boy?'

'Didn't he tell you that he had a kid?'

Elli folded her arms and tilted her head back. She looked at Philby from behind the bar with a smile turning her mouth.

'Very funny,' she said.

'What?' he asked.

'Get fucked.'

'What?'

'As if he's got a kid.'

'I don't know.' Philby frowned at Elli. 'That's what she said.'

'Bullshit. You're just saying that because I told him I had a kid.'

Philby looked at Elli, then grinned.

'That's right, I forgot you said that. How weird that you said you had a kid, when he really did have one.'

'Piss off. He doesn't have a kid.'

'I don't know. I'm just telling you what she said.'

'If he had a kid, why did he sprint down Collins Street when I said I had one?'

'Yes, and I'd know the answer to that. I don't know, Elli. Maybe he didn't want to get involved? Maybe it was too tricky? Who knows. You'd have to ask him that.'

'I can't believe he's got a kid.' Elli tugged at the bottom of her bra and wriggled her boobs up, up, up, into the cups, until they were filled to overflowing.

'I'll take their bill over,' she said.

Philby looked over at Tristan and smiled.

They watched Elli move from behind the bar and kitten over to the table where Minnow and the girl were sitting. They watched Elli stand there, about to put down the bill folder. They watched her startled look as she suddenly recognised who was sitting at the table. They watched her tilt her head towards her shoulder and point to herself, reminding Minnow who she was. They watched Minnow's face open up eagerly as he recognised Elli and started chatting to her. They watched her kneel down beside him and keep talking, while the girl sitting at the table with Minnow crossed her arms, and clenched her teeth in a visible jawlock. They watched Elli watching Minnow. Minnow's elbow was resting on the table, his whole body turned towards Elli. Minnow and Elli both laughed, Elli's head flicked back slightly. The other girl didn't laugh. Minnow introduced his date to Elli. Tristan could see the girl say 'pleased to meet you', although she didn't look pleased to meet Elli at all. Elli stood up, and bent over to rub her knees. Minnow slipped his eyes down the front of her top, quickly, like two darting hands, then looked back up into Elli's face.

Elli came back over to the bar with the bill folder in her hand. All the other tables were now empty.

'So?' Tristan asked. 'What did he say?'

'He said the brioche was lovely.'

'Yeah. And?' said Philby.

'He told me about his new job. He's working at some radio station.'

'What about his kid?'

'I couldn't ask. How could I say I knew he had a kid? "Philby told me you've got a kid. So, have you?" I don't think that would go down all that well.' Tristan took the bill folder and swiped Minnow's Visa card.

'S. Sinclair? What's his name again?'

'Minnow.'

'What's the S stands for?'

'Don't know. Spunk from the looks of it.'

Elli took the Visa slip over to their table. She came back to the bar.

'So how long's he been with her?' Tristan asked.

'No, she's not his girlfriend, she's just a friend from work.'

'Sure,' said Philby.

'She is.'

'Right,' said Tristan.

'Well, that's what he told me.'

'Of course he would.'

Elli turned towards table nine as Minnow and Mona got up to leave. She clicked her tongue.

'He's really nice, you know. I don't know why I said I had a kid that night. I fucked it up big time.'

'Don't worry about it,' said Philby. 'He looks like he'd be a bit of a player to me.'

'Do you think?' asked Elli.

'Definitely.'

Minnow came over to the bar.

'It was nice seeing you again,' he said to Elli. 'See you later.'

'Yeah, you too,' she said.

Mona was standing near the door. As Minnow went over to Mona, she put her arm around his waist. Tristan locked the door after them and came back over to the bar.

'Not his girlfriend, you don't reckon,' he said.

'Yeah, but he didn't put his arm around her, did he?'

Tristan raised his eyebrows, but didn't answer.

He could hear Chris in the kitchen, washing up the saucepans. The till was silent. The restaurant was quiet. No more smiling at fuckwit customers. He cranked the music right up. Philby lined five glasses up on the bar and opened a bottle of Hugo's. Elli went into the office and sorted out the roster for the next week. Philby reset the tables for the next day, and Dave and Tristan sat at the bar discussing next month's menu. Elli came back out and had a sip of her wine, before going into the bathroom and getting changed out of her uniform. Dressed down and cashed up, she sat back at the bar divvying up the tips while she had her wine.

'Do you guys want to go down to The Martini Den after this?' she asked. That's when the phone rang. Dave looked at his watch and grinned at Philby, who had finished setting, and was now sitting.

'That'll be the handbrake,' Dave said, referring to Philby's girlfriend who always rang around this time, asking when he'd be home.

Philby picked up the phone.

'Hi baby,' he said.

'Oh. Hang on,' he said. It wasn't his baby at all. 'I'll just get her for you.'

He held the phone out to Elli.

Elli frowned and looked at him. 'Who is it?' she mouthed.

He didn't answer, just held the phone out for her to take.

'Hello?' she said. The boys watched her on the phone. 'Oh, hi,' she said, pushing her hair back behind her ears, then pulling it back out again, raking her fingers through it. 'Yeah, actually we were just talking about going there in a minute, for a drink,' she said, looking over at the boys and opening her eyes wide. 'Great. I'll see you there then,' she said. 'Bye.' She hung up the phone, took a deep breath, and bit her bottom lip. She breathed out and took a sip of her wine.

'Finish up,' she said, as she put her glass down.

'What's happening?' Philby asked.

'We're meeting Minnow at The Martini Den in about fifteen minutes.'

'With the girlfriend?'

'No,' Elli grinned, pulling a strand of hair across her mouth. 'She's gone home.'

Tristan grinned at Elli and shook his head.

'Scored,' he said.

'You betcha,' Elli replied.

Chapter 10

Mona shits Minnow. He was tempted to graffiti it across the wall of the car park at work so that she got the message. Mona fucking shits Minnow up the wall, and could she please piss off and leave him alone? Please? Thank you. It had been two days. Two days since he'd told her he didn't want to see her anymore. Forty-eight hours of her hassling him, ringing him, crying to him, bothering him, pestering him, turning up at Crush to see him, driving past his house, ringing him at home, abusing him, hanging up.

It had started three nights ago when he'd met up with Elli again. Driving home from The Tea House, Mona had sat beside him, lips shut cold and tight. He didn't ask her if she was okay because, to be honest, he didn't give a shit. They got back to her place. And then she started. Whining. Whinging. Complaining. Asking questions. Demanding answers. Crying. Sobbing. God, she looked bad when she cried. She was quite pretty usually. But sitting next to him in the car, with her nose dripping like a gutter on a rainy day that hasn't had the leaves cleared out of it, she didn't look young and pretty. She just looked bloody awful, and snivelly, and puffy. Minnow looked through the windscreen, waiting patiently for Mona-by-name-Whinger-by-nature to finish, so that he could go and ring Elli before she left work. He knew Elli would be a bit longer in the restaurant, clearing up, getting things organised for the next day — glasses, cutlery, crockery. Probably have a drink afterwards. But he and Mona had been the last ones to leave the restaurant, so Elli wouldn't be there a whole lot longer. He needed to call her before she left, otherwise it might be hard to contact her.

He knew what it was like when he'd worked in that restaurant in London. He never got a message if someone rang for him and he wasn't there. There were bills and order forms and crap all over the desk, so any phone messages for staff would just disappear, and eventually disintegrate under the pile of paper paraphernalia. He wanted to speak to her, see her, catch up. She was a total babe. He couldn't believe he'd let that kid thing bother him so much. He'd gotten used to the whole single-parent thing now. Of course, there'd always been Kate, but now, at work, he chatted in the tea room with some of the mums, and they weren't boring. They were okay. Some of them were even interesting. And you'd think that they'd be shithouse at their jobs, but they weren't. In fact, some of them were good. He shouldn't have let Elli being a mum freak him out so badly. He should have gotten to know her before he had decided whether or not to split. He just needed to get Mona out of the car, then he'd call her.

At first things had gone well with Mona. The whole dad thing was a major turn-on for her. And even though he thought he'd blown it when Kate said he couldn't take Lochie to the picnic, it had all worked out rather well in the end. He'd arrived to pick Mona up, and she'd had the full picnic catastrophe happening in a clichéd wicker basket.

Ham, chicken, avocado, dips, biscuits, chips, apples, pears, chocolate and all this other shit — he couldn't even tell you what it was.

Mona had looked at him curiously when she saw no Lochie. Maybe even a bit suspiciously. But Minnow had told her he'd decided it was a little premature for Lochie to meet a new woman, 'you know, seeing as his mum only just split a couple of months ago', and Mona had just about gotten tears in her eyes, and said to him, 'God, you're amazing,' and he knew it was even better that he hadn't brought Lochie along, than if he had. If he'd brought Lochie with him, he'd have had to be really careful that Lochie didn't say too much, and that Lochie remembered to call him Dad. And in hindsight, it probably wouldn't have worked out all that well. Not having Lochie there was perfect.

Mona had whispered to him that night in her bed what a fantastic father he was, and what a great guy he was, and how he was the sort of person she could easily fall in love with. Minnow should have known then that she was going to be an absolute boa constrictor. And he had always known he wasn't going to see her for long. She was pretty and had this really hot bod, but she wasn't that interesting. And she giggled a lot, even when he wasn't saying anything particularly funny, and she was young, and while that could be a good thing, he wasn't interested in being a Professor Higgins to her Eliza Doolittle.

So they sat in the car after they left The Tea House and he'd told her that it was best they stop sleeping together because he didn't think it was right 'for Lochie, you know how things stand, what with his mum gone. We're still getting used to living together, two boys. I think it would be best if

I just concentrated on him for a while'. He should have known she wouldn't take it well. But he hadn't expected the magnitude, her sitting there, crapping on about how much she liked him, and how she wanted to keep seeing him, and for fuck's sake, she was really boring him. He had tried to give her the message a couple of times by looking at his watch, but she just didn't seem to pick up on the subtleties. So he finally turned to face her, and said, 'Look, I need to get home for the baby-sitter. I really can't discuss this anymore tonight. We can talk about it later, if you need to, but right now, I've gotta go.'

And she'd looked at him, not understanding at all — selfish, stupid girl — and started bleating on again about her and him, and how she'd fallen in love with him, and all this other bullshit. Minnow had sighed, and looked at his watch. It was nearly 45 minutes since they'd left the restaurant. He really had to get going. Chances were Elli wouldn't even be there anymore, and it was all stupid Mona's fault. He leaned his elbow on the steering wheel and turned to Mona.

'Listen,' he said, enunciating very clearly to make sure she understood, 'I have to go. I can't keep sitting here, listening to you. I've got a baby-sitter to pay. In fact, it's costing me $10 an hour to sit here with you. I've got to get home. The relationship thing isn't happening between us, I don't know why, maybe it's the age difference. Maybe it's because I've got a kid. I don't know. We can still be friends,' *Iqbal,* 'and maybe we can go to the movies one night soon. But for now, I've really gotta go.'

Mona sat there, looking at her hands which were offering each other moral support in her lap. Minnow leaned forward and looked into her face to make sure she understood. She looked back at him shyly, drippy nose, swollen eyes, pasty skin, and then — gross — she moved forward to kiss him. He kissed her with do-not-enter lips, and moved back. He looked at his watch.

'Honestly Mona, I've got to go. Please. We can talk later if you'd like.'

Maybe if he spoke really kindly to her, she'd get out of his fucking car. He mentally made a sticky note and stuck it to the very front of his brain. It read 'Never, ever, ever, again. Mona is a no-go zone.'

Finally, she got out of his car so he could drive off. He pulled over around the corner, rang The Tea House, and organised to meet Elli.

As he walked through the door of The Martini Den his shoulders dropped back into position. He hadn't realised how tense Mona made him feel. But now he was here, sitting, waiting for Elli, he felt surprisingly good. He breathed the atmosphere in, deep into his body. He breathed out slowly, getting rid of any last Mona droplets that might have been circulating in his system, and ordered a beer.

The door opened and he turned towards it. He recognised a couple of the guys from The Tea House. Behind them walked Elli. She looked hot. Again, Minnow couldn't get over how not like a mum she looked. He stood up and smiled as the five of them came over.

'Hi,' he said.

'Hi,' she said back, then introduced 'a couple of the guys I work with, Tristan, Philby, Dave, and Chris.'

Minnow sat there patiently listening to them all talk, adding his own bits, asking them all questions, but really wanting them all to piss off so that he could have Elli to himself. He watched her talking to them, the way she looked in each of their faces as they spoke, listened to everything they said, interested in each of them, including him. God he wanted to fuck her so badly. He felt the warmth of his erection, and had to lean forward and think about Warren Bourke, Human Resources Manager, for a couple of minutes to quell his stiffie. He wanted to be home, with Elli flat on her back, and him flat on her front, all of their clothes on the floor. Then he had to think about Warren again for a couple of minutes, his head of pube hair in particular, and that awful poster he had behind his desk.

Philby turned to Minnow. 'So, how old's your little boy?' he asked.

Minnow looked with surprise at Philby.

'My little boy?'

'Yeah, I heard you speaking about your kid to that girl you were having dinner with. Sorry, I'm a shocking eavesdropper. So, where's he tonight?' Minnow couldn't believe it. He hadn't planned on bullshitting to Elli about having a kid, but now the five of them were standing, watching him, waiting to see what he had to say.

'Actually, that's all bullshit. I only said it so I could work part-time hours at my job. It also worked brilliantly well for getting Mona in the sack.' Yeah, that would go down really well, especially seeing as Elli was a mum herself.

So he said, 'He's at my mum's. She sometimes looks after him for me.'

'I didn't know you had a kid,' said Elli.

'Yeah, well, I suppose it just didn't come up,' except for the fact that Elli had mentioned having a kid herself, so that sounded like fucking crap. 'How's your kid going, by the way?'

Tristan, Philby, Chris and Dave all turned and looked at

Elli. Elli looked briefly down at the ground, then straight back up into Minnow's eyes.

'She's really well,' she said. 'How's your new job going anyway? Which station are you working for again?'

Work talk. Just her and him. The two of them. Chatting. She turned her body towards him. Away from the others. Shouldering them out of this conversation. Tristan and Dave said they were going home. Chris and Philby said they were too. Minnow looked at Elli.

'What do you want to do?' he asked.

She smiled at him, and he imagined exactly what she wanted to do.

'I wouldn't mind one more drink,' she said.

'Same.'

'Okay, well we'll see you guys later then,' said Philby.

'Bye,' said Dave, Tristan, and Chris.

And then it was just the two of them. Minnow and Elli. Elli turned to face Minnow when the others had gone.

'So,' she said.

'A needle pulling thread,' he replied.

She grinned at him. 'What happened to your friend tonight?'

'She was tired. She just wanted to get home.'

'Fair enough. But she's not your girlfriend, you said earlier.'

'No, just a friend. Although I think I might have to stop seeing her as often as I have been, because I think she might want it to be more.'

'Oh. How awkward.'

'Yeah.'

And speaking of awkward, there was this silence that followed. A hole. A gap. A weirdness that didn't feel weird until they were halfway through it, and suddenly Minnow felt this retrospective uncomfortableness that overwhelmed him. He wished he smoked. If he smoked, he'd light one up now, offer the pack to Elli, fire up the conversation with a fag. But he didn't, so instead he picked up his beer and downed it. He picked up Elli's empty glass and stood up to go to the bar, but an attack of the responsibilities struck him and he said to her, 'Or do you need to go? What time do you need to be home for your kid?'

Elli looked startled, as if she'd had a really good stare happening, and then Minnow had wiped his hand through her vision, shattering it.

'Um, well, yeah, no, I'd better not have a drink. I'd better get going.'

'Who looks after your daughter when you're working?'

Elli cleared her throat. She frowned. 'There's this, ah, woman. A neighbour.'

'Right. Does she have kids as well? Do you swap baby-sitting or something?'

'Yeah. Yeah, it works really well.'

'What's your daughter's name?'

Elli frowned again. 'Her name? She's called Daphne.'

Minnow smiled. Elli looked so shy talking about her daughter. Probably because he'd been such an arsehole last time she'd said she had a kid. He tried to open her up a bit, signal to her that he didn't mind that she was a mum. 'That's a great name. Does she look like you?'

Elli looked to the side, then down. 'No, not really. I think I'd be right in saying we look quite different.'

'Does she look more like her dad?'

'Um. It's hard to tell.' Elli picked up her bag. 'Anyway, I should get going,' she said.

Walking to her car, Minnow wanted to put his arm around Elli, but decided against it. Instead, he put his hands in his pockets and hunched his shoulders up against the night.

They got to Elli's car and he watched her get her keys out. She looked up at him and smiled. He stepped forward and put his arms around her, just like that first night.

'Déjà vu,' he said.

'Yeah,' she smiled. 'This all seems pretty familiar.'

He looked down at her, so pretty, so sexy, so shy.

'Would you mind if I kissed you?' he asked.

Elli bit her lip. She looked straight into his eyes, deep, searching for who he was. Minnow looked down at her mouth, avoiding her eyes.

'I'm not sure,' she said, a smile lurking.

'Should I give it a go?' he asked.

'Can't hurt,' she said, tilting her face, her mouth, towards him.

He leant down and kissed her. He pulled her body as close to him as he could. He wanted to step inside her skin. This time he didn't try to conceal his erection. He didn't think about Warren Bourke, Human Resources Manager, at all. Not once. Not for one second while he was kissing Elli did he think about Warren Bourke. He just thought about Elli. He smelt her skin, he breathed deep and smelt her hair. She seemed completely unaware of how totally gorgeous she was. He could barely breathe. He didn't even ask if he could go home with her.

And the next day when Doug said 'Jevuker?', instead of saying 'Nahbeda', Minnow just said, straight out, 'No'.

Chapter 11

Last night Daphne had sex for the first time. Well, not for the first time ever obviously, for godsake. Although, when she came to think about it, it was for the first time ever in a bloody long time. Since she and 'The Bastard' had split up, in fact. But it was for the first time ever with Gus. Daphne didn't go in for one-night stands, or first-night sex. Not that she was a prude, it's just that she had discovered over a few one-night stands and first-night sex, that she didn't really like instant, nice-to-meet-you-how's-about-a-bit-of-a-romp-right-now-this-very-second sex all that much. She didn't enjoy it. She didn't find herself getting turned on. She just found herself getting all self-conscious and trying really hard to enjoy it, trying to concentrate on the task at hand, but all the while thinking about who was this guy, and what was she doing in bed with him, she didn't even know him, and did he deserve to have sex with her that easily (probably not), and would he think she was a slut because she'd hopped in the cot with him so easily (probably), and shouldn't she have a bit more self-respect (definitely), and all these thoughts would swill around in her head, making it really hard to enjoy the moment when there was so much else going on at the same time.

She remembered the last time she'd had a one-night stand. She'd been overseas at the time with Amy; this was before Amy was married, before she was going out with Hugh even, and way before Daphne had started going out with 'The Bastard', so it was a very long time ago, but it put her off casual sex forever. She had been lying in bed with this American guy in Greece — should have been romantic but it wasn't — trying to enjoy the sex, trying to put out of her head all the things that were whizzing around (chattering monkeys they call it in meditation, 'the chattering monkeys of your mind'). Anyway, so she's lying there, and this American guy is on top, going for it, and she's trying to relax, trying to enjoy it, trying to ignore the chattering monkeys, and he starts speaking. In. Time. With. Each. Thrust. And he's saying to her, 'What. You. Need. Is. A. Damn. Good. Fuck.'

Truly. That's what he said. In. Time.

'What. You. Need. Is. A. Damn. Good. Fuck.'

And she'd lain there, with him on top and her underneath, legs akimbo, thinking, 'What kind of fucking arsehole are you, you fucking fuckhead,' and she'd said to him, in response: 'That sounds great. Do you know where I could get one?' and then just lay underneath him, waiting for him to answer.

'What?' he'd said, stopping for a moment, hoisting himself up onto his elbows. And she'd put her most bored expression on her face and repeated herself.

'I said, that sounds great. Do you know where I could get one this late at night?'

An uncertain smile rose to his mouth. He gave a bit of a laugh. But she'd looked at him stony-faced.

'I'm serious. Get off me.'

He lay on top, looking into her face. He didn't move. It seemed he wasn't one hundred per cent sure if she was serious or not. She nodded at him.

'True story. I'd like you to hop off now. I've gotta find myself a damn good fuck, and there's no point hanging around here, 'cause it's obviously not going to get much better than this.'

'What if he'd bashed you up?' Amy had said the next morning, laughing into her coffee.

'I know,' Daphne had said, 'it was probably a really stupid thing to say, but I couldn't believe this guy was saying that to me. It totally grossed me out.'

So thanks to Humper, the gross-me-out-American fuckwit, Daphne had never indulged in casual sex again. Since that night, she had only ever had sex with a guy when she knew him well, liked him a lot, and felt comfortable enough with him not to have the chattering monkeys anti-meditation thing happening.

'The Bastard' had been one of those guys. And now Gus. Last night. They had been out to see some short films at the St Kilda Film Festival (two were good, the others were shithouse, but that's the kind of strike rate you expect with short films), then they'd gone for a drink at Crush, and finally home for some hot nook-wa.

'So how was it?' asked Elli, barely moving her mouth because her face mask had been on for fifteen minutes and was now crack-dryable.

Daphne delicately lifted the cucumber slices off her face and looked over at Elli.

'None of your business.'

'Piss off, of course it's my business. The walls in this flat aren't that thick, and I was home last night.'

'Omigod, did you hear them?' asked Amy, who was lying on a couple of cushions on the floor, french-polished toenails drying, mud mask hardening, and cucumber slices freshening her eyes.

It was Saturday, but not pyjama day. This Saturday was beauty day. Of course, every girl is familiar with beauty day, and it barely requires explanation, but for the sake of any novices, actually, fuck it, if you need beauty day explained, you need to glam-up a bit.

So. Where were we? Daphne was on the couch, cotton-wool balls between each of her Revloned toes, a mask painted thickly on her face, cucumber slices 'reducing puffiness around the eye area', according to *Cosmo*, and a 'rejuvenating' mask slathered on her hair. Elli sat on the chair opposite Daphne, Revlon Espressoed toenails resting on the coffee table, a hard-as-a-brick jojoba and aloe vera mask on her face, and cucumber slices on her eyes à la Daphne. And Amy was on the floor, the third wise beauty monkey.

'Yes, I certainly did hear them,' said Elli. 'A number of times.'

'Gross,' said Amy. 'That's my brother-in-law you're talking about.'

'So,' said Elli. 'How was it?'

Daphne smiled and bit her lip.

'It was nice, actually.'

'Nice?' asked Elli.

'Very nice.'

'Does nice mean nice, or good, or a bit boring but the raw material is there to work with?'

Daphne grinned.

'No. Nice means fucking fantastic, actually,' she said. 'No improvements necessary.'

Elli grinned, and her faced cracked like old plaster. She got up and walked into the bathroom.

'Don't say anything while I'm in here,' she said, splashing water on her face to loosen the mask. 'I can't hear a word.'

'So. Any more where that came from?' asked Amy, with a cheeky smile.

Daphne raised an eyebrow. 'Any more what?'

'Sex, of course.'

'I'm pretty sure there will be.'

'What was that?' Elli called from the bathroom.

'I said I'm pretty sure we'll be seeing each other again.'

'God,' said Amy, 'this is going to be weird. You going out with Hugh's brother. Imagine when you start coming to family dinners and things. Imagine if you guys get married. It'll be so much fun.'

Daphne rolled her eyes, which doesn't communicate very effectively when there are slices of cucumber on top of them.

'I think it might be a bit premature to talk about marriage,' she said.

'Don't tell me you're talking marriage already,' said Elli, walking in on the end of the conversation. 'I think it's a bit early for that, isn't it?'

Daphne laughed. 'Absolutely.'

'So, when are you seeing him again?' asked Elli, settling back onto the chair, nail file in hand to start the manicure process.

'He said he'd call later today and we'd do something tonight.'

'He's keen,' said Amy.

'Definitely,' said Elli.

'Has he said anything to Hugh?' Daphne asked Amy.

'Well, not really, sort of. You know what guys are like. He

told Hugh you'd been out, and he said he'd had a great time with you, but he's kept pretty mum since your first date.'

'Has Hugh asked him anything since?' asked Elli.

'No. He's hopeless with goss. I've told him before to ask all the questions, but he never does. He says it's none of my business.'

'But Daphne's your friend. How can it be none of your business?'

'I know. Exactly.'

'And it happened because of your dinner party. Of course it's your business.'

'I agree,' Amy shrugged. 'I said that to Hugh, but he just ignored me.'

'Bastard,' said Elli.

'He is,' said Amy. 'He's the worst husband I've ever had. Anyway,' Amy continued, looking at Elli, 'that's Daphne and Gus sorted. How about you and that guy from the other night. What's happening there. Has he called? Are you going to see him again?'

'Minnow?'

'Yeah.'

Elli made big sweeping moves with her nail file, then a series of small, quick moves, then more big, broad brush strokes.

'Nah, that's hopeless. He thinks I've got a kid.'

'Has he called?'

'Yeah, he rang me yesterday at work. But it's too complicated.'

'Because of the kid thing?'

'Yeah.'

'Just tell him,' said Daphne, joining in the conversation, 'that you made it up. Say it was a joke.'

'Yeah, that would be fine if I hadn't kept it going the

other night. But he asked me about my kid, and I just stood there and lied. I could have told him it was crap, but I didn't. I should have, because it was the perfect opportunity, but I think I was just blown away by finding out that he has actually got a kid. If he didn't have a kid I'd have just told him it wasn't true, but I didn't say anything, and now it's too embarrassing to tell him.'

'So what are you going to do?'

'Nothing.'

'What did he say when he called?'

'He asked me out. Next week,' Elli lifted a shoulder, then dropped it back into position, 'one night.'

'Which night?'

'Well, it wasn't anything definite. He said he'd call. He asked me what nights I was working.'

'So are you going to go?' asked Amy.

'Nuh.'

'But you should,' said Daphne.

Elli went back to filing her nails — short, sharp sweeps — and biting her lip.

'It's too hard. He's really nice, I really like him, but it's too hard. I'd sit there feeling sick about not telling him that I don't really have a kid, and it would be awful.'

'Well, just tell him,' suggested Amy.

'It's different. You know, if it was you and Hugh, you could tell him.'

Amy smiled. 'I think he'd have noticed by now.'

'Yeah, but I mean, if you'd told a lie to Hugh, you could tell him, and talk about it, and that's what happens when you're married. But I've only met this guy a couple of times. If I sit down with him and tell him it's crap, he'll just tell me to piss off. He'd think I was a nut.'

113

'You are a nut,' said Daphne.

'You know,' said Amy, 'he didn't tell you the first night that he had a kid. He kept quiet about it. And you told him you had a kid but you don't really. So it's almost like you sub-consciously knew that there was a kid issue happening between you, even though you didn't know he had a kid.'

'Right?' said Elli.

'Well, it's kind of spooky, don't you think?'

And at the word 'spooky' a fist hammered on the door. A heavy bang, bang, bang.

'Who'd that be?' Daphne asked Elli.

'Dunno. Bags not,' said Elli.

'Bags not,' said Daphne.

They both looked over at Amy. She lifted her cucumber slices off her eyes a fraction, glanced at them both, then put the cucumber back in position.

'Well, I'm not,' said Amy. 'It's not my place.'

'You have to, then,' said Elli to Daphne.

'Why?'

'I bagsed not first.'

Daphne hmphed, and got up to answer the door. As she walked down the hall, she could see this big square head through the stained glass of the front door.

She opened the door. And fuck me, standing there was this big, ugly, Juicy-Fruit-chewing motherfucker, who looked like he'd escaped from some outer suburb and was walking around inner city Elwood, unleashed, just banging on people's doors. She tilted her head and squinted at him. He looked kind of familiar, but she couldn't quite place where she'd seen him. And then her blood rushed down towards her feet, leaving the rest of her body chilled like some kind of human daiquiri. He was the guy she'd seen in the park that night, staring at the flat. The guy who'd come into her work, who Sally had described as 'this real thuggy looking meat-head in a flannelette shirt'. And he must have followed her home, because now he was standing on her doormat, in his flannelette shirt, glaring at her through his piggy little eyes. A thug. A thuggy looking meat-head. A powerful, strong, scary, prison-escapee-meat-head thug, standing on her doormat in his flannelette shirt. She went to shut the door, but he stuck his foot in the way. Her heart ricocheted wildly around her chest. A scream got stage fright and lay wheezing pathetically at the base of her throat. The jojoba and aloe vera mask felt dry and hard on her face, making her feel even more uncomfortable. She could scarcely breathe.

He looked at her grimly, not saying a word.

Chapter 12

Jacinta lay in bed with Minnow. He gently scratched her name up the length of her back. Jacinta watched his chest breathe deep as he filled his lungs with post-coital satisfaction. He was shorter than she had remembered from the first night. And a bit stockier. And he had a slight American accent too, which she hadn't realised at first. But he was handsome, she'd remembered that right, and he wore nice clothes. And she remembered the sense of humour. That was the same. One thing did puzzle her though. His chest was much hairier than she remembered. Normally she didn't like men with hairy chests, and she thought it would be something that would have stuck in her mind from the first night. But it wasn't until the second time they were together that she noticed how hairy he was. Then again, she was so trashed the first night they met, it's amazing she remembered anything about him at all.

The night he'd come to pick her up and take her out, she was dead nervous. She'd only had a vague impression of what he was like, no specific details hung in her head. Blond, slim, handsome, tall. That was it. When the door had knocked out a stranger's arrival, she opened it wondering how accurate her drunken stupour would be. Now, of course, after they'd been seeing each other for, it was over three weeks now, she could tell you everything about him. Eyes? Green. Nose? A bit hooked, but only slightly. Mouth? Soft with a little dip in the middle. Chin? Strong and a bit jutty-out.

She could tell you that he was a stock-market analyst (but she couldn't tell you what that meant exactly). She could tell you that he wore boxer shorts, not jocks. That he liked cricket a lot, but liked footy more. That he rode a Ducati which was 'way better than a Harley Davidson'. That he loved going to see bands. That his friend Kate was going out with the lead singer of Frenzy. That he got severe belly-button lint, probably because he had such a hairy chest. She could tell you that hairy chests were actually incredibly sexy, not a turn-off as she'd once thought of them. That a hairy chest was really manly. That the hair on a man's chest led the mind (and eye) wandering down past the chest. Down, down, down. She didn't know why — it just seemed to happen that way. She could describe with absolute precision the expression he wore when he was having an orgasm. The way his face would screw up in pain and concentration, a noisy, noisy, noisy lead-up and then aa-aa-aa-aa, like the soft ticking over of a just-turned-off car engine as he slumped over her heavily.

Minnow came over at least three nights a week, and she expected that pretty soon he'd start taking her out and introducing her to his friends.

'I don't want you to meet them just yet,' he had said one night recently. 'I want to keep you all to myself for a bit longer.'

He'd told her all about them though. Doug and Kate. Kate's boyfriend, Ben. Bardo, Thommo, Ringo, Robbo and

Wilbur. Marco, whose art exhibition she'd been at the first night she'd met him.

Steven had told her to go to the exhibition. He had told her Marco was an 'up-and-comer' and that he wanted her to choose a couple of paintings and buy them for him.

'But I don't know anything about art,' Jacinta had said to Steven.

'Just choose two. For me. Just think to yourself, "what would Steven like?" and buy them. I can't come down from Sydney, so I want you to go for me.'

The thing was, Jacinta didn't really feel that she knew Steven well enough to select two paintings for his collection. She didn't know the type of décor Steven had. She didn't know whether he had white walls or coloured ones. Or wallpapered ones, for that matter. She certainly didn't know what sort of art he liked. And she didn't know what Marco's paintings were like, what style they were. They might have been Australian landscapes, and she hated Australian landscapes, so if that's what they were like, she wouldn't have a clue which one was best. Which was the best buy. Which one was the smartest choice. Much less which two.

But she went anyway, with Sarah. Thank God there were no landscapes. Two paintings immediately appealed. The first was of a fat man riding a donkey, painted in a naïve style. She liked the way the fat man wasn't holding the reins. The reins were just flopped loosely around the donkey's neck. It was like the fat man didn't need to cling on to anything to feel totally in control. He was just looking forward, along for the ride. The second painting she really liked was of the Madonna and child. There was something very serene about it, very innocent, very childlike.

But she didn't buy them. She bought two others which she didn't like as much, but there was brains behind her purchases. One was the biggest and most expensive, and the other was the smallest and most expensive, so she figured she was right on the money with those two. The big one had lots of fish swimming in all different directions. Heaps of fish. Bright ones. Dull ones. Grey ones. Psychedelic ones. Fat. Thin. Tiny. Enormous. Even some which were just bones, a skeleton, no flesh. All bordered by a very thin, finely striped eel. She supposed it was quite good. The other one, the small one, featured an abstract nude, not much detail, more shapes and colours than a body. In each of the hands was a fork and a spoon. It was very deep.

With a red dot beside each of Steven's new paintings, Jacinta and Sarah went to the bar to get a glass of wine. And another. And another. And just one more. On their fifth reconnaissance up to the bar Jacinta stood next to a guy, blond, slim, tall, and handsome. He'd smiled over at her and said, 'Partner.'

Jacinta had looked up at him and said, 'What?'

'You're my drinking partner. Every time I come up here, you're here.'

'Am I?'

'Yep. Which means you must be really pissed, because I am.'

Jacinta had laughed.

'I'm Minnow,' he'd said.

The phone rang. 11:57 p.m. Jacinta answered it quickly to stop Minnow being hauled away from the edge of sleep.

'Hello?' she whispered.

'It's me,' said a deep, manly voice.

'Oh hi. Hang on, I'll just go into the other room.'

'Why?'

'I want to grab a glass of water. Hang on.'

She put the phone down and looked over at Minnow. His eyes were closed.

'Who's that?' he asked.

'A friend. She always rings at ridiculous hours. Go back to sleep.'

Jacinta went into the kitchen, shut the door, and picked up the phone.

'Hi. How are you? How's Sydney going?'

'Not that well actually,' he answered.

'Oh,' Jacinta said, suddenly flushed and anxious. She felt like she'd done something wrong. That there was a problem and she'd caused it. She always felt that way when he rang. She never felt comfortable speaking to him on the phone. When he was in Melbourne and they were having dinner it was pleasant enough. He'd just talk about himself mostly. She could just nod, and smile, and act interested. Go back to her place and have sex with him. But on the phone the dynamic always changed. It was like she was the secretary and he was the boss. No. Like she was the receptionist and he was the boss and she'd fucked-up some pissy little something, and now he was furious with her. Even when he was being nice to her, she felt like that.

'Why?' she asked. 'What's happened?'

'Do you know a Daphne Templeton?'

Jacinta thought for a moment. Daphne Templeton?

'No. Don't know her. Who is she?'

'She's an art director at an advertising agency.'

121

'Nuh.'

'She lives with Elli Pirelli.'

Jacinta felt the whump of a vacuum slurping all the air out of her lungs.

'I know Elli.'

'Yes. I know you do. You've been having a word to her, have you?'

'What? About you? About us?'

Jacinta felt fear surge through her system, a physical emotion. No wonder they said animals could smell it.

'Yes.'

'No. Of course not. Why?'

'Well you must have been.'

Jacinta frowned. 'I haven't. I promise. I hardly even speak to her. I mean, I speak to her, but just about work and stuff. Nothing personal. She knows nothing about me, and I know nothing about her. We're just workmates.'

There was no way she'd ever let it slip to Elli about her affair with Steven. It wasn't really something she was particularly proud of. Admittedly, there were some aspects of it she enjoyed — the flat she lived in, the credit card he'd given her, the car leased in his name which she drove. Some parts of it were good. She may even have hinted to Elli a few times about gifts he'd given her. Like her watch. And her earrings. But she'd never said his name. A couple of times Elli would ask 'how's your man going?', but Jacinta had never told her who he was. Or what he did. Or how rich he was. She'd definitely never said his name. At least, maybe she'd said 'Steven'. But never Rickards. Definitely never Steven Rickards. Definitely. Definitely not. She didn't think.

'Well, it's very unusual, because she knows we're having an affair, and she and her friend have decided to blackmail me.'

'What do you mean?'

'You know. Blackmail? Extortion?'

Jacinta narrowed her eyes. He could be so rude when he wanted to be. Treating her like some dumbfuck bimbo who was happy to have sex with him and take his gifts, and if he wanted to treat her like shit, he could. He really pissed her off sometimes. She could picture him sitting on the other end of the phone, probably still wearing his suit, probably still at work (no wonder he had affairs, he never saw his poor wife), his pasty face reddened, licking his downturned mouth every so often, and stinking of expensive wine.

'Yes, I know what extortion is. But what do you mean she's blackmailing you? What did she say?'

'I haven't spoken to her. She sent me a letter. I'll read it to you.'

She could hear him unfolding the paper.

'"Dear Mr Rickards, we are two young girls who are broke, but who don't want to be anymore."'

'Shit.'

Jacinta started chewing one of her fingernails.

'"We believe that if someone gave us a bit of a hand financially, we could really do great things. We feel that the amount we're talking about would hardly be small change to someone of your immense wealth, but for us, it would make a real difference to our circumstances. We are looking for a benefactor to subsidise our financial independence. Whatever you think is a fair sum. Next time you're in Melbourne, please feel free to drop by and say hello."'

'But how do you know it's a blackmail letter? She doesn't say anything about me. It could be about anything.'

'I think it's pretty clear. It doesn't have to be spelt out.'

Jacinta sat silently. Unsure what to say. Steven started talking again.

'At first we didn't realise that it was because of you. One of my men tried to dig up what they might know. He spent a bit of time on Daphne, thinking she had maybe learnt something about one of my business dealings that we might want to keep quiet.'

'Like what?'

Steven ignored her. Just kept on steamrollering through the conversation.

'So we looked into a few things, the accounts she worked on, research she may have done, but came up with nothing. She's an art director, she doesn't know anything.'

'Okay.' It seemed the safest thing to say.

'But of course, she does know something, doesn't she? Because she lives with Elli Pirelli, and Elli works with you, and Elli knows about us.'

'Well, I don't know how she knows,' Jacinta said.

She could hear the whine in her voice, the insincerity, the panic, but she really didn't know how Elli would have found out.

'Maybe,' Jacinta suggested, 'because you sometimes come into the restaurant when you're in town, she's put two and two together.'

Steven was silent at the other end. Finally he said, 'She must be very clever.'

'I promise, I've never told her anything.'

She could hear him breathe heavily into the phone. Breathe in. Breathe out.

'And you know nothing about this letter?' he asked.

'No. How would I know about it?'

'This is the first you've heard of it then?'

'Yes, of course.'

'It seems very strange,' he said.

'What do you mean? What seems strange?' Jacinta could feel her heart pounding in her throat. 'Are you asking if I'm in on it?' She could hear her voice rising. She knew she sounded guilty. She knew it. If she was him, she wouldn't believe her. She'd hear the hysterics, the 'guilty conscience', and she'd think 'you're a fucking bullshitter, and you are totally in on it'. She felt herself spinning out of control.

'Are you asking if I'm blackmailing you?' Her voice was rising, but then she remembered Minnow in her bed, asleep, but maybe not, so she lowered her voice a degree. The hysterical edge remained.

'Are you suggesting I'm blackmailing you about having an affair with me?' She knew he was not the man to be on the wrong side of. She knew he had 'men' who did 'jobs' for him. 'What would be the point? Why would I do that? You give me money. You pay for my flat. You've given me a car. Why on earth would I do that? I cannot believe,' she said, her words welling with tears, 'that you would even think that for a moment. I mean, fuck, what sort of person do you think I am? You must really like me a lot. I had no idea how low your opinion of me was. I mean, God.'

He didn't answer immediately. She wanted to hang up, but she was too scared to. She worried that by slamming the phone down, it would seem another example of guilt. Instead she stayed on the phone, waiting for him to answer.

'Okay,' he said, 'calm down. It doesn't matter anyway. My man paid them a little visit this morning, I assume I won't be hearing from them again.'

Jacinta felt giddy. What did that mean? I won't be hearing from them again? Were they dead? Maimed? Gone on a long trip?

'What did he do? Are they alright?' she asked, her voice rising.

She could hear Steven breathe heavily into the phone.

'Don't be so melodramatic,' he said, 'of course they're alright. So long as they understand this is the end of it. Do you understand?'

Jacinta shrugged her shoulders, suddenly tired, worn out. Nothing she said would make him believe her. He would never believe that people weren't snakes. That's the way he did business, and he assumed everyone else was the same.

'Whatever,' she said.

'Needless to say, I'd appreciate you being a bit more discreet from now on.'

She shook her head, and narrowed her eyes. She didn't answer.

'Jacinta. Do you understand?'

She clenched her jaw tight to prevent any more than just the smallest 'yes' to escape.

'I'll be down next Monday,' he said. 'We'll go out.'

'I'm working next Monday,' and I'd rather not see you, you fucking arsehole, she didn't say.

'Well, get it off. I'm coming down.'

She said nothing. He sat waiting. Finally, she said, 'Yeah, okay.'

She hung up the phone. What a prick. What an arsehole. Pig. Acting like she'd been blabbing to Elli. She didn't know how Elli had found out, but it certainly wasn't from anything Jacinta had said. Maybe Elli had seen them out one night together. Maybe she'd seen them driving around. Maybe she'd heard through a friend of a friend. Maybe more people knew about their affair than Jacinta realised.

Jacinta went and climbed back into bed. She chewed her cheek as she lay there, thinking how it would be next time she was working with Elli. What was she supposed to do? Pretend that she didn't know about the letter? Act like normal? Ignore it? Ignore the fact that the fucking moll, the fucking, fucking, bitch-slut-moll, was blackmailing Steven? One of Australia's richest and most powerful men.

'Are you okay, Jac?' Minnow asked sleepily, rolling towards Jacinta and laying his arm across her stomach.

'Yeah, fine.'

He opened his eyes and propped himself up on his elbow. He looked down into her face. 'Sure?'

'Yeah, no, it's nothing. Don't worry about it.'

He continued looking at her.

'It was nothing,' she said. 'Forget it. Just this friend of mine from Sydney. She's a bit annoying sometimes.'

Minnow leant over and kissed her softly. Both cheeks, her forehead, her mouth. He propped himself back up on his elbow and stroked her brow, trying to wipe away any problems she might have.

'You're too pretty to frown,' he said.

Jacinta smiled. He leant over and kissed her again. And again. She put her arms around him, and scratched down his back with her fingernails.

Fuck Steven, thought Jacinta, as Minnow continued kissing her deeply. She was over this mistress shit. She didn't even particularly like him. It had been kind of exciting at first, the dinners, the presents, the flat was a spin-out, the car, the credit card. But tonight, after that phone call, she was over it. She'd move out. She had Minnow. She didn't need Steven anymore. It was morally wrong anyway. And he was an arse-hole. She'd just find a new place to live, buy a car. Jacinta thought for a minute more. Maybe the smart thing to do would be to wait a couple more months, save some money, buy her clothes for next season, then give him the flick.

He could go fuck himself.

But for the moment, for the moment, the only fucking that was going to happen was with Minnow. And her. Right here. Right now.

Chapter 13

Daphne stood at the door of the flat. Her in trakkie daks, pink singlet, and jojoba and aloe vera mask. Him in a flannelette shirt, blue singlet, and two big fists hanging like legs of lamb, either side.

She felt fear racing through her body, making her feel hot. There was no question of fight or flight. She was all set to fly. Only problem was he had his great bloody foot wedged in the doorway, preventing her from shutting him out. Stopping her from flying back into the lounge room. Stopping her from screaming out. Stopping her from doing anything at all. Just stopping her. She stood perfectly still. Dead still.

Dead. Still.

Dead. Not yet.

'This is for you,' he said, and handed her an envelope.

She frowned and took the envelope from him. Her blood slooshed rapidly back up through her body.

'What is it?' she asked.

'It's what my employer thinks is reasonable,' he said.

And then he took his foot from inside the doorway, turned from her and lumbered back to his plug-ugly car.

Daphne looked down at the envelope in her hand. She couldn't possibly imagine what was inside. It was one of those yellow, bit-bigger-than-normal-type envelopes. Whatever was inside was bulky. Not massive, but certainly bigger than your standard one-page letter. No company name on the front. Nothing on the back. Daphne was crawling with curiosity. Itching to open it. She couldn't possibly imagine what it contained. So she put the envelope down on the hall table, and left it there.

She walked back into the lounge room.

'I remember when I first met Hugh,' Amy was saying, 'and I know we both said things that weren't exactly the truth. That's just the way things are when you first start seeing someone. Everyone knows that.'

'Yeah, but not exactly telling the truth is a bit different from saying you've got a kid.'

'True.'

Daphne sat down.

'Who was at the door?' Elli asked. She'd finished filing, and was up to the undercoat.

'You remember that guy. The one who asked about me at work, and was over in the park that night?'

'Omigod,' Amy raised her cucumber slices and looked up at Daphne. 'What did he want?'

'He gave me an envelope.'

Amy sat up and took her cucumber off.

'What's in it?'

'I don't know. I haven't opened it yet. I'm trying to work out what it could be first.'

'Why don't you just open it?' asked Amy.

'Well, because then I'd know, and I like not knowing for a little while, trying to guess what's inside.'

'She always does this,' Elli said to Amy. 'It's so annoying.'

She turned back to Daphne, 'Have you left it on the hallway table?'

'Yeah.'

'Go and get it, so we can at least have a look at it.'

Daphne went back into the hallway and grabbed it. She handed it over to Amy, who turned it over, looked at the back, turned it back to the front, looked at it again, then handed it over to Elli.

'Shit,' said Elli, 'I've fucked up my undercoat. Come on, open it,' she said to Daphne. 'I want to see what it is.'

'I will in a minute. I just want to think about it a bit more.'

'Maybe it's a job offer? Maybe he's a head hunter?' suggested Amy.

'Somehow, I don't think so. He didn't look like he was from a recruitment agency.'

'Just open it,' said Elli.

'I will. I'm just thinking.'

'Do you want me to open it for you?' asked Amy.

Daphne scoffed. 'As if. It's not that I don't want to open it. It's just that I like anticipating opening it. If I just straight out open it, then I can't anticipate opening it.'

Amy looked at Daphne. 'Whatever.'

Amy felt certain there was something a bit more witty or clever or funny or appropriate or insightful she could have said at that point, but nothing came to her so she just settled on 'whatever'.

Daphne finally took the envelope from Elli and looked at it. She turned it over, opened the seal, looked inside, looked over at Amy and Elli, giggled, then looked back inside the envelope.

'Omigod,' she said.

'What?' they both asked.

'Omigod,' she repeated and tipped the contents onto the table.

'Omigod,' they both said.

Money. Bundles of fifty dollar bills. Ten bundles. And a note.

'Received your letter. Believe this is a reasonable amount. Trust you won't bother me again. Steven.'

'Shit,' said Amy. 'Steven who?'

'It doesn't say,' Daphne said and looked at Elli. 'How many Stevens did we have?'

'I don't know. I'll grab the list.'

Elli left the room.

'Is this from that letter you guys sent off?' asked Amy.

'Must be,' said Daphne.

'Fuck, that's brilliant. I can't believe someone actually sent you money. Unreal.'

Elli came back into the room, carefully holding the *BRW* List of the Hundred Richest Men and Women between her first finger and her thumb. She kept her other three nails well away. She didn't want to ruin her undercoat any further. Elli sat down on the couch next to Daphne and went through the list, counting.

'There's 17 Stevens. It could be any one of them. What does the letter say again?'

'It just says "Steven".'

'Nothing else?'

'Nuh.'

'What should we do? Should we ring each Steven on the list and ask if it was them?'

'I don't think we can do that. It would be a bit strange to

speak to all the others and for them to say "no, I didn't give it to you".'

'Yeah, that's true.'

Daphne picked up the note and read it again. 'He must want to remain anonymous,' she said. 'I mean, it's not on a letter-head, or anything like that. Maybe he's shy. Maybe he does good turns like this all the time, but doesn't want to get the pub-licity. Otherwise everyone would be writing to him, asking for money.'

'Hang on,' said Amy. 'You wrote to all those people didn't you?'

'Yeah.'

'But none of them would know you wrote to anyone else. He probably thinks he's the only one you wrote to. He probably thinks he can sign it Steven, because he assumes you know exactly who he is already.'

Daphne nodded. 'That'd be right. Definitely. Because nowhere on the letter do we say we're sending it to the others. So we certainly can't ring and ask any of them if it was them, because whoever it is might get mad if he finds out we sent it to 99 others. Don't you think?'

'Yeah, that's true,' said Elli. 'But if he assumes we know it's him, don't you think he might think it's a bit rude if we don't write to say thanks?'

'Yeah, he might,' said Daphne.

'Probably,' said Amy.

'But we can't,' said Elli.

'No,' Daphne and Amy agreed.

'Unless,' Daphne said, after a moment, 'we wrote a letter to all the Stevens saying thank you for . . .' Elli and Amy watched her. Waiting. 'I don't know, thank you for, receiving the first letter we sent them. Maybe?'

Elli and Amy looked unconvinced.

'I don't think so,' said Elli.

'How about if we write a letter, just being really vague, but carefully worded so that the one who sent the money knows we're saying thank you, but the others think it's just a normal letter. What do you think about that?'

Elli chewed her lip. Amy frowned.

'But what would it say?' asked Elli.

'I don't know. Maybe if it said something like, thank you for, I don't know, being a good corporate citizen, and Australia needs more of you?'

Elli frowned. Amy chewed her lip.

'Mmm,' said Elli.

'Maybe,' said Amy.

Daphne watched them both carefully.

'Well? What do you think?'

Amy sucked her lips. Elli pouted.

Finally, Elli said, 'Yeah. No, I don't think so.'

This, by the by, is a classic example of a yeah-no-ism. A yeah-no-ism occurs often in everyday speech, and can mean a number of things. In this case, of course, it means no, but by preceding it with a 'yeah', Elli is hoping to not hurt Daphne's feelings. Other yeah-no-isms can be the 'yeah, no' spoken abruptly as in 'yeah, I heard what you said but I absolutely, totally disagree with you' and the 'yeah? no?' spoken hesitantly, hoping to guess at the correct answer simply by answering 'yeah' and 'no' at the same time. There are others, but these three are the most common.

'You don't like it?' said Daphne, well aware of the subtleties of yeah-no-isms.

'Well, it's not that I don't like it, I just think it might be a bit weird for the other 16 who receive it, and the one who sent us the money would also think it was weird. It just sounds a bit strange.'

'Well, maybe the wording is wrong, but the general idea, I think, is quite good.'

'Yeah, maybe. Anyway,' said Elli, turning to the cash on the table. 'What are you going to do with yours?'

'How much is it?' asked Amy.

'Five thousand, I think,' said Daphne. 'Hang on, I'll count it.' Daphne counted the money.

'Yep, five grand.'

'That's two and a half thousand each.'

'God, that's bloody fantastic!' said Amy.

'It's not bad, is it,' said Elli.

'What are you going to do with it?' asked Amy.

'I don't know,' said Elli.

'I'm going to buy some clothes,' said Daphne. 'I mean, two and a half thousand, it's good, but it's not really heaps, is it?'

'No, it's not exactly Tattslotto,' said Amy.

'No, but still, it's not bad.'

'No, it's not bad at all.'

'Better than a kick in the head.'

'Definitely.'

'Not as good as first division Tattslotto though.'

'No, you're right there.'

Amy and Daphne looked at Elli.

'What about you?' Amy asked. 'What are you going to spend yours on?'

Elli tucked in the corner of her mouth, and dropped her head towards her shoulder. She put her thumbnail in her mouth and started chewing thoughtfully.

'Your undercoat,' said Daphne.

'Shit,' said Elli, looking at her nail. 'No, don't panic anyone, the nail's fine.'

Daphne smiled. 'So, what do you think? You wanna go buy some clothes?'

'Yeah, maybe,' said Elli. 'I mean, in some ways I think we should just blow it on clothes, because it's not really ours anyway, we didn't do anything for it, so we should just blow it.'

Daphne nodded. 'Yeah.'

'But then, in some ways,' Elli continued, 'I think, because it's been given to us, it's a bit silly for us just to blow it. You know, it's like an opportunity has been given to us, and we shouldn't just throw it away.'

'Well, yeah, I know what you mean,' said Daphne, 'but it's not really like we've been given this massive opportunity. It's only two and a half thousand each. It's not like we can start our own company or something.'

'No,' agreed Elli.

'I mean, we can't even buy a good couch for two and a half grand.'

'You know,' said Amy, 'you'd even be struggling to buy a really good coat for two and a half.'

'Yeah, that's true,' said Daphne, 'like, say, a Prada coat would be at least four thousand.'

'Yeah,' said Amy, 'even a good handbag from, say, Hermes would cost more than that.'

'Mmm,' said Elli. 'But there are still heaps of things we could do with two and a half grand.'

'Like what?'

'Well,' Elli shrugged her shoulders, 'for instance, we could buy a ticket overseas.'

'Yeah,' said Amy and Daphne.

'Or, um, a jetski.'

Daphne frowned and looked at Elli.

'A jetski? Where did that come from?'

'I don't know. I was just thinking about big things we could buy.'

'I reckon a jetski would be more than two and a half thousand anyway,' said Amy.

'We could start some kind of little business together.'

'Doing what?'

'I don't know. You're an art director. I'm a graphic designer. Okay, I'm a waitress, but I'm trained as a graphic designer. Maybe we could open up our own agency.'

'With five thousand dollars?' Daphne asked.

'Maybe.'

'I don't think so,' said Daphne. 'Anyway, I don't want to start up a business. I like where I work. And having your own business would be a drag.'

Elli picked up the Revlon Cappuccino and leaned forward. She splayed the fingers of her left hand on the coffee table and started painting with her right.

'Well, maybe it would be good to go overseas. Remember when we first wrote the letter, that's what we originally said we'd do. Remember?'

Daphne thought for a minute.

'Yeah,' she smiled, 'it'd be good to go away. That'd be fun. Where would we go?'

'How about Paris,' said Elli. 'I've always wanted to go to Paris.'

'Yeah. We'd still have to save up some spending money, but yeah, I'd be up for a trip overseas.'

'We don't need to save spending money. We could work over there.'

Daphne sat back and crossed her legs up on the couch.

'But I don't want to go over for a long time. I like my job. And not that I want to live my life according to whatever guy I happen to be with at the time, but I don't necessarily want to say to Gus, "I'm going away indefinitely. See you when I get back." I'd be happy to go for a holiday, but not for months.'

Daphne uncrossed her legs and stood up.

'Actually, I can't really talk. My face is seizing up.'

She walked into the bathroom.

Elli looked over at Amy.

'What do you think?' she asked.

'Do you know what?' said Amy. 'If I was you, I'd go over-seas. Work there for a while, have a good time. You like your job, but it's nothing you can't come back to in a year. And you're not seeing anyone, so there's nothing tying you to Melbourne. But I can see why Daphne doesn't want to.'

'Yeah, same,' said Elli, now painting the nails on her right hand.

Daphne came back in from the bathroom, freshly scrubbed. No mask.

Amy stood up.

'I think I need to do that too,' she said, and left the lounge room.

'So, what's the score?' asked Daphne.

'Well, I think I might go away. Go and live in London for a while. I could hook up with Simone and David.'

'Yeah, that'd be fun,' Daphne nodded. 'So I suppose that means I'd need to get someone else to move in here?'

Elli looked at her.

'Yeah. I suppose. No one too fun though. I wouldn't want you to like living with them more than me.'

Daphne smiled.

'I wouldn't. Don't worry.'

Elli's eyes lit up.

'Hey, maybe you could get Gus to move in. What do you think?'

Daphne screwed up her nose.

'Nah, I don't think so. It's a bit early-days for that.'

Amy came back in looking fabulously mask-free, and stood in the doorway of the lounge.

'So what's happening?' she asked.

'Well,' said Daphne, 'Elli's going overseas, and I'm going shopping.'

'Perfect. Let's go have a drink. I think a vodka martini is in order.'

'Ooh,' said Elli, shaking her hands to dry her nails, 'that sounds brilliant. I just have to do my topcoat, and I'm ready. And get changed. And finish my toes. And then I'm ready.'

'Can I borrow something from one of you guys?' asked Amy. 'I can't be bothered going home.'

'For sure,' said Daphne. 'Just have a look and choose whatever. Except not my red skirt. I think I might wear that.'

'Okay,' said Amy, going into Daphne's bedroom. 'I might call Hugh as well, and tell him where we are,' she called out.

'You know what,' said Elli, looking up at Daphne from her topcoat application, 'if I go overseas, it's also perfect, because it means I can keep seeing Minnow for the next little while, before I go, and then when I leave, it's over, no drama.'

'What?' said Daphne. 'And not tell him you don't really have a kid?'

'Um. Probably.'

'Yeah, that's not a bad idea. Except what if the more you see him, the more you like him, and you start writing to each other while you're away, and then you come back home and want to go out with him again? Then you'll have to tell him.'

'I don't think so,' said Elli. 'I'm sure that's not going to happen. Remember the first night I met him? I didn't really think he was my type anyway. It's just for a bit of fun. Just until I go away.'

Daphne looked down at her toenails.

'Hmm,' she said.

'In fact,' said Elli, brightening, 'it's absolutely perfect.'

She finished her topcoat and looked at her shiny nails.

'Perfect.'

Chapter 14

Minnow didn't want to fuck Elli. He didn't want to score with her. He wanted to lie in bed next to her. He wanted to gently kiss her, fully clothed. He wanted to taste her mouth and smell her skin. He wanted to feel her against him, hear her breathing softly, close his eyes and see her clearly in his mind. He wanted to hold her head, kiss her face, gently, gently. He wanted to lie beside her, fully clothed. He wanted to smell her, and taste her, and watch her.

And then he wanted to fuck her. He wanted to be inside her. He wanted to feel her in the most extreme ways possible. He wished he'd never had sex before, that this was the first time. He didn't want the memory of any of the others in the bed with him and Elli. He wanted to make love for the first time in his life. He wanted to fuck her. He didn't want to fuck her. He wanted to lie in bed with her and show her exactly how he felt about her. He wanted her to feel his feelings. He wanted her to hear, with the very lightest touch, a whisper of a touch, the words he couldn't say. Because he'd never said them before. To anyone. He'd never even imagined saying them.

He didn't even like feeling what he was feeling. He didn't trust it. It didn't feel familiar. It felt different. It felt wrong. But not bad wrong. Good wrong. Like everything he'd felt before now was harsh and brittle. He'd thought it was normal the way he'd been before. The way he'd always kept a fair whack of distance between him and any girl. He had liked being in control. Not relying on a chick. Not particularly caring if they stayed or went. The thing was, they always stayed. He was always the one to say let's leave off. He'd always been the dumper, and he had liked it that way. But with Elli it was different.

He racked up the balls and handed the cue to Elli. She placed the white ball just to the left of centre. He smiled to himself. It wasn't like she'd misjudged, it was like she figured that was the best spot. After many games of pool, she'd done her maths and calculated that the optimum possie for the primo opening was just to the left of centre. She smashed the white ball, a mini explosion shattered the triangle at the other end of the table, and number 11 went into the end pocket.

'We've got big balls, you've got small ones,' she said, grinning at the two guys they were playing.

That's those two guys there, the gigantors with the motorbike leathers and the ZZ Top beards. The ones who look like they haven't yet been fully integrated back into society, after their lengthy stay in one of the state's bluestone establishments. They laughed at Elli, but Minnow had the uneasy feeling that if she said any more of that shit, he was the one they'd beat up.

Elli and Minnow were at The Espy in St Kilda, one of Melbourne's finest institutions. A favourite. When developers had tried to fix it up, there were protests and petitions and outrage and eventually, victory by the residential Davids of St

Kilda over the Goliath of big business. The developers backed off and the carpet remained sticky from years and years of beer swilling and beer spilling, the paint kept its patina of cigarette smoke, the booths maintained the red vinyl benches with graffiti on them, and that was just the way the locals liked it.

After a few games of pool, Minnow and Elli went into The Kitchen for dinner, out the back of The Espy. Candles stuck in old wine bottles, crowded tables, and the guy behind the counter so stoned, he kept forgetting to take their money. Elli grinned at Minnow from across the table, swizzling her vodka and tonic with a straw. She'd just told Minnow that she'd bought a ticket for overseas. She'd bought it a couple of days ago and was leaving in less than a month's time, she wasn't sure how long for. Minnow had felt this ball of something unpleasant knot up in his stomach.

'Well that's fantastic,' he'd said quietly.

Elli continued grinning at him, not noticing the disappointed tone of his voice and told him where she planned on going.

'First up I'm going to England, because some friends of mine live over there at the moment. Simone and David. So I'll stay with them for a while, not sure how long, then I think I'll go to Italy 'cause I've got some rellies over there.'

'Are you taking Daphne with you?'

Elli stopped, took a breath. She looked up at him.

'Yep.'

Minnow felt the knot in his stomach unballing and whamming up inside his brain, a brilliant idea flowering.

'You know,' he said, 'I might come and meet you over there.'

Elli's eyes opened wide.

143

'But what about your job?' she said.

'I'll take time off.'

'But you might not be able to get it. You only started a couple of months ago.'

Minnow shrugged.

'Fuck 'em, I'll quit. I'm not that into it anyway. I'd much rather go back overseas with you and Daphne. And I've got these really good friends in England, you'd love them. They're excellent fun.'

'What about Lochie?' she asked.

Minnow looked down at the table.

'I'm not sure,' he said.

And Elli stopped grinning and leant over her vodka and tonic, trying to spear the lemon with her straw.

Minnow watched her. She was so lovely. So gorgeous. So different from any other girl he'd ever been with. He didn't want to fuck it up with her. He knew he had to be honest with her. This crap with Lochie, it had been a work thing, it wasn't supposed to spill over into his social life. He had to tell her. He had to tell her he didn't really have a kid. He knew she'd be mad. She might even not want to see him again. But once he told her, he could explain what had happened, how it had been a mix-up. That he knew it was wrong to lie at work about having a kid, but it hadn't seemed that bad, and it was a good way to get reduced hours. And he would never have lied to her about it, never, except that guy she worked with asked him about it, and he just couldn't say it was a bit of a yarn because then they'd have all thought he was an idiot, but he could tell Elli now, it wasn't too late, this was only the third time they'd been out together since the other night, and she'd be fine. She'd understand. Look at her. She'd be absolutely cool with it.

He looked into Elli's eyes. He was going to steamroller his way through this part of the conversation. Tell her before he lost his nerve. He had a slug of his beer, took a deep breath. But Elli looked away. That was all it took for him to stop in his tracks. He looked at her, bent his head down to try and fall into her line of vision. She looked away again. Shit. He'd blown it. By saying he wanted to meet up with her, he'd fucked up. It was too much too soon. She wasn't ready for it. He sounded too keen. She had a kid to consider. She didn't want to have every idiot that fell in love with her traipsing around Europe after her. She wanted to have a holiday with her child. Just her and Daphne. Not her and Daphne and Minnow.

'Is everything okay?' he asked.

Bile rose up his throat.

'Yeah, it's fine,' she answered.

But he could tell it wasn't. Usually, in this type of situation, he wouldn't push it. He'd just leave whoever she was to sulk and then when she was ready to buck up, she could. Because usually, in this type of situation, he didn't really give a shit what the problem was. But this time, he did care. He asked again. He pushed her.

He said, 'I can tell something's wrong.'

He waited for her to say it. To say she didn't want him to come overseas with her. Didn't want him to meet them over there. Wanted to have time with her kid and her friends, not her kid and her friends and him. He waited for her to say something. But she didn't.

'Elli,' he said. 'I'm sorry. Maybe it all seems a bit rushed. A bit sudden. I don't mean I want to come overseas with you guys straightaway. I just mean that maybe, in a couple of months, I could join you. We wouldn't even have to travel together the whole time, if you wanted to be alone, just the two of you.'

Still she said nothing.

Minnow's shoulders dropped. 'Or maybe there's something else.'

Like maybe she wanted to dump him. Maybe she was over him before it had even begun. It would serve him right. There'd been plenty of times when he'd flicked a girl after only a couple of nights. Kate called it his 'dresses on a rack' approach.

'It's like when I'm looking at dresses in a shop,' Kate had said, more than once. 'I go up to a rack and flick through, maybe stopping quickly at this one or that, but then I keep flicking and usually end up leaving the shop without having even tried something on.'

'Unfair,' Minnow had said, 'I always try them on.'

Kate had raised her eyebrows.

Minnow hadn't really thought much about it. Kate was always sticking up for the girls he dumped, like they were all some kind of gigantic sisterhood network. But now, with Elli opposite him, about to tell him to piss off, he realised that what Kate had been saying was right. That he didn't really give any of them much of a chance. And this is what he wanted to say to Elli, that she hadn't even given him a chance. But he couldn't say anything. He could only watch Elli, as she tried to spear her lemon.

'Actually,' Elli said quietly, stopping the lemon thing, but not looking at Minnow, 'there is something.'

Minnow looked back down at his beer. He felt blank.

'It's about Daphne,' she said quietly.

Minnow looked up.

But Elli didn't continue. She'd stopped. She was looking past Minnow and frowning at someone standing just to the right of his shoulder, behind him. Minnow hooked his eyes along Elli's line of vision and turned to face the person.

'Hi,' said the girl.

Minnow looked back down at his beer. He shook his head and sighed.

'Mona,' he said in a voice that he hoped conveyed what he really wanted to say, which was 'piss off'.

'This is a coincidence,' said Mona.

'Really?' asked Minnow, in a bored voice.

'Yeah. Well, actually, I saw your car parked out the front so I guessed you were in here, but I was coming here anyway with a couple of friends. We're in the front bar.'

'Good.'

Mona looked down at Elli.

'Hello,' she said. 'You're the waitress, aren't you?'

Elli smiled up at Mona. 'Yeah, hi. I'm Elli.'

'Yes, I remember. So,' Mona said, turning back to Minnow, 'how's it going? Where have you guys been tonight?'

Minnow folded his arms across his chest.

'Just playing pool,' he said.

'How did it go? Did you win?'

Minnow unfolded his arms and rested his arm on the back of his chair, facing Mona fully.

'Look, Mona,' he said, 'we're just about to have dinner. We might come out and see you in the front bar later on. Okay?'

Mona bit her fingernail, and looked at it.

'Yeah, alright.'

She stood at their table for another couple of seconds before moving towards the door. Minnow turned back to Elli. He could feel Mona out of the corner of his eye, watching them both. He concentrated on Elli, and felt Mona move into the other room.

Elli raised an eyebrow and smiled at Minnow.

'Well, it was great catching up with her again,' she said.

'Yeah, sorry about that,' he said, leaning forward on the table. 'Anyway, what were you about to say?'

Elli shook her head. 'No, nothing. It was just something, but really it's nothing.'

Minnow smiled. God she was fuckable.

'No, you wanted to say something. You started saying. It was something to do with Daphne. Do you think she wouldn't want me hanging around with you guys when you're travelling?'

Elli grinned and bit her lip.

'No,' she said, 'I'm pretty sure the Daphne I know would love nothing more than to travel around Europe with you and me. The more the merrier is her motto.'

'Well, what is it then?'

Elli put her hand on top of his.

'Nothing.'

Minnow looked over at her.

'I promise,' she said. 'It's nothing. You and Daphne would get on really well. It's not that I think there would be a problem.'

'You know,' Minnow said, taking ahold of Elli's small hand, 'I know the first night we met I was a complete fuckwit about you having a kid. I shouldn't have just bolted. I don't know why I did it.'

Elli shifted in her chair and looked down at his hand holding hers.

'Forget it. It's fine. It was totally understandable. Let's talk about something else,' she said.

'No, but I want to talk about it. I want you to know that you can tell me anything. I won't bolt the way I did that first night. Really. You had something to tell me, but then you decided not to.'

Elli looked up into Minnow's eyes. He felt her questioning him, on the brink of telling him something. Telling him something about Daphne. Something. Maybe she hadn't told Daphne yet that she'd met a guy. Maybe Daphne had a problem with her mum dating. Maybe Daphne really badly wanted her mum and dad to get back together, kids often did, and the thought of some other guy with her mum would really piss her off. Elli picked up her glass and finished her drink.

'What I had to tell you is this,' she said, and she took a deep breath. 'I need another voddie.'

Minnow smiled.

'That's not what you were going to say.'

'It is. Well, I didn't need a new one then, because I hadn't totally finished, but now I really do need another one. Look. Empty.' And she pointed to her glass.

'Yeah, you're right you know,' he said, smiling, relieved.

Like, he was really happy to have the heavy conversation if she wanted to, he wanted to be there for her, he wanted her to see that she could talk to him, that he wouldn't run, but if she didn't want to talk about it, that was fine too. He felt a hot flush as he realised that he'd been so close to telling her about Lochie. He'd been about to tell her, he had been about to say it was all bullshit, but she was still so vulnerable, so unsure of him, if he'd told her tonight she would have totally spun out. He'd wait a couple more weeks, then he'd tell her.

He came back from the bar with their drinks. Elli raised one of her eyebrows in Minnow's general direction.

'Anyway,' she said, 'what's with Mona? She looked a bit pissed off to see me with you. Is she still hung up on you?'

And Minnow told Elli how he tried to avoid Mona as much as possible at work. How lucky it was that he spent most of his day out of the office. How she kept ringing him on his mobile when he was about to go into meetings with clients.

'She's a full-on nightmare. These friends of mine, I've told you about Kate and Doug, haven't I? They call her The Bunny Boiler,' said Minnow.

'Really?'

'Yeah. You know *Fatal Attraction*? Where Michael Douglas has that affair with Glenn Close, but he's married, so she boils his kid's bunny.'

Elli smiled. 'Omigod. I hope she's not like that.'

'She is. She's a pain in the arse. She keeps driving past my house. I answer the phone at night and she hangs up. It pisses me off. Even if I wasn't with you, I wouldn't be going there again.'

Elli looked puzzled. 'But you told me you were just friends.'

'Oh, yeah, well, we were. I mean, one night we were together,' fuck, he'd forgotten he told Elli he hadn't been with Mona, 'and I think it meant more to her than it did to me.'

'Oh,' Elli put her head in her hand and looked straight at Minnow. 'What a drag. You know, you'd think she'd have a bit more respect. For herself, apart from anything else. And also, it's not like you don't have enough on your plate. You know, looking after Lochie, on your own, working — it's not like you need another thing to worry about.'

Elli took a sip of her vodka.

'Poor Minnow,' she said. 'You're just too too handsome. The girls can't keep their hands off you, can they?'

He smiled.

'No. It's a drag.'

He grinned at her. She smiled back.

'So how's Lochie doing, anyway?'

Minnow poured some beer down his throat, drowning any words that may sabotage him.

'Yeah, good,' he answered.

'Does he see his mum at all?'

And then the guy behind the counter called out Minnow's name, and put their meals on the bench for Minnow to come up and grab.

'I'll get them,' Minnow said to Elli, as she went to stand up. She sat back down again.

Minnow picked up their two meals. He was going to tell her about Lochie. Definitely. Absolutely. No question. Maybe tonight they could just have a really good night, and then next time they went out, he'd tell her. Next time. Not tonight. Next time.

Chapter 15

Elli knew all about signs from God. When she'd been with Ben, when they were still together this is, she'd tried to ring him this one particular night from work, but there was no answer. That was a sign from God that she shouldn't speak to him. But she'd ignored the sign. She kept dialling the number over and over again. When he eventually picked up the phone, she remained calm. For about a second. Then she raved on and on, had a go at him, where had he been, had he been with a girl, that sort of thing. The next night, he told her it was over, that they weren't right together, that she should move back in with her parents until she found some-where else to live. God had given her a sign, but she'd ignored it.

Meeting Minnow that first night, she should never have said she had a kid. But she had. And then last night, just as she'd been about to tell him that Daphne wasn't really real — well at least, she was real, but she was about 23 years older than he'd been led to believe — Mona had shown up, and it was a sign from God that she shouldn't tell Minnow the truth. Minnow wanted to come overseas with her. Minnow liked her that much, he wanted to toss in his job and travel with her. But he thought she had a kid. He thought she was a single mum, not a single girl. And when she'd been about to tell him, God had sent a sign, warning her not to say anything.

Minnow had been through enough shit from women. His ex had dumped Lochie on him. That girl Mona kept hassling him. He probably didn't have much faith in women. If she told him she had lied, that she didn't really have a kid, it may be the last straw. He might never be able to trust women again. It wasn't just about him and her. It was about him and all women. It was bigger than the both of them. And other clichés.

Minnow. She really liked him. Liked him a lot. He made her feel the way she'd felt when she was a little girl, when her dad lived at home. Before her dad had moved out, and moved in with that bimbo from his work. After her dad had moved out, he hadn't loved Elli as much anymore. He didn't see her as much. And Minnow would be the same once he discovered what she was really like. Who she really was. He liked her at the moment because he thought she was someone else. Someone different. Not her. He didn't really know her. He thought she was a mother, and that was something he could relate to, because he was a dad himself. He thought they really had a strong bond. But once he realised that she didn't really have a child, that she was a liar, he'd be disappointed and she couldn't bear to see him looking at her the way she knew he would, once she told him. She was going to stick with the original plan. Keep seeing him until she went overseas, then finish it up. Not tell him the truth. Not tell him she didn't really have a kid. Keep it fun, keep it light, keep it going for a bit longer, and then she'd be outta here.

She wouldn't say a thing. She'd stick to the plan.

'Well, what are you going to say?' Amy asked. 'He's going to want to know why he can't meet you overseas.'

'I don't know. I won't give him a forwarding address. Once I leave, I'll stop contacting him.'

'You can't do that,' said Daphne. 'That's mean.'

'Bad luck. Guys do it to girls all the time.'

'Why don't you just tell him?' said Amy. 'I mean, if he doesn't want to see you anymore, that's fine. You'll go overseas and have a fabulous time on your own. But at least if he knows the truth, he's got the opportunity to forgive you. If you just stop seeing him, you're not giving him the chance.'

It was too hard to explain.

'I can't. Maybe I'll tell him I can't see him anymore because I think it would be too difficult travelling with my kid and his kid.'

Amy laughed and started shuffling the deck of cards.

'Just tell him the truth,' she said. 'You're only going to make it worse if you tell another lie. Imagine if he found out that you didn't really have a kid? Then not only would he be pissed off that you'd lied to him about that, he'd also be pissed off that you'd used a non-existent kid as a reason to break up.'

'Maybe you're right,' Daphne said to Elli, taking the well-shuffled cards from Amy. 'Am I supposed to shuffle them too?' she asked Amy.

'Yep.'

'Right about what?' asked Elli.

'Maybe you're right not to tell him. Remember you said the other night you thought it wasn't meant to be. Maybe it's because you're going away, and because you know you'll only be with him for a short time, that you're falling for him. Do you know what I mean? It's kind of like a holiday romance, but in reverse because you're not on holidays yet.

Maybe if you weren't going away, if you were going to keep seeing him like normal, you wouldn't be so keen. It might be kind of a "because you know you can't have him" type thing. You know? So when you go away, you can just tell him it's over. You're not interested. You don't need to go into great detail. Just say the combination of the two of you isn't working.'

But it was working, that was the thing. It was working so well. Elli knew that Minnow brought out the best in her. He didn't make her feel insecure. She didn't feel threatened by other girls. That chick Mona, for example. Mona obviously liked him, wanted to be with him, but Elli didn't feel fragile about that. It was fine. Mona could want Minnow all she liked, Elli didn't care, because she knew Minnow was totally absorbed in her. He kept saying he wanted to spend as much time with her as possible. He rang her each day at work, wanting to catch up. And they would have been seeing each other all the time, except Elli had to keep saying she couldn't go out because of her kid, that he couldn't come around to her place because of her kid, that she couldn't stay at his place because of her kid, that he couldn't stay at her place because of her kid. And she didn't even have a stupid kid.

It had been two weeks since she'd met up with Minnow again, since he'd come into The Tea House with Mona. He kept saying, 'I'd like to come around to your place. I really want to meet Daphne. I'm sure we'd get on really well.'

But the Daphne he wanted to meet was seven years old, and the Daphne she lived with was a bit older than that. So she had to keep saying she didn't think it was time yet, that Daphne wasn't ready, that Daphne may feel threatened, and all the time she kept making things worse and worse. If she'd just told him the first night, well, the second night, or even the third night, it would have been fine. But she hadn't, and now she was stuck with this lie that kept getting bigger and bigger, and it was going to take an international jumbo jet to haul her out of it.

Daphne finished shuffling and set the pack of cards down on the table. She picked the first card off the top, and laid it, face up, on the table. Amy raised her eyes and looked at Daphne.

'The Lovers,' she said.

'Well there's a surprise,' said Elli, rolling her eyes.

Amy, Elli and Daphne were in Amy and Hugh's lounge room. Amy had a scarf tied around her hair, and every necklace she owned was draped around her neck. Daphne had lit some incense sticks to set the mood, but Amy had butted them out pretty much straightaway, because they stank. Elli had fired up a joint instead, to lend the required exotic aroma to the room.

'Okay,' Amy said. 'Hang on a tick, I've got to find what the book says.'

Amy had bought the tarot cards and instruction book at Camberwell market a couple of Sundays ago. She flicked through the book, and finally stopped somewhere near the middle.

'So, The Lovers card means a few things. It says that the hovering angel there, that's Cupid. He's given your relationship his seal of approval. And see how that guy is kneeling at the girl's feet? Well, that means Gus adores the ground you walk on.'

'Good so far,' said Daphne. 'What else does it say?'

'It says that in exchange for the loyalty and love you give

157

him, he will be generous and protective, and is prepared to make some big sacrifices on behalf of his love.'

'Well, yay for me,' said Daphne.

She turned over the next card.

'Three of Cups,' said Amy. 'Now wait a sec, because the order they're in also means something.'

She flicked through the book.

'Okay,' she said, finally.

'You're a bit slow,' said Daphne. 'No offence.'

'Alright, this card next to The Lovers card is very good. It symbolises abundance. Not necessarily financial wealth, but abundance of life. Maternity, happiness.'

'Oh my god,' said Elli, elbowing Daphne. 'A baby.'

'Shit, I hope not,' said Daphne.

She bit her lip and turned over another card. The King of Coins.

'This one shows that Gus is practical, down-to-earth, skilled in practical techniques and traditional crafts. That kind of goes with him being a gardener I suppose. And it says he is loyal, trustworthy and patient with an — ahem, just one moment please while I quote directly from the bible — an "inborn wisdom that enables him to achieve material success and even amass great wealth. He is devoted to those he loves. He is slow to anger, but implacable towards those he hates".'

'Does that mean he has a bit of a temper sometimes?' asked Daphne.

'I don't know,' said Amy. 'I suppose so.'

Ten of Coins.

'This is another good one,' said Amy. 'It means there's this real contentment thing happening between you two. You're both going along the same path. Laying down foundations together.'

Her last card was the Queen of Swords.

'Okay, this one's showing that you are highly intelligent . . .'

'There must be some kind of mistake,' said Elli.

'. . . with a complex personality. You are alert to the attitudes and opinions of those around you. But you must make sure that you keep your feet on the ground. That you don't become so rapt in Gus that you lose yourself.'

Daphne had a drag of the joint and looked at the cards. She nodded and passed the joint over to Amy.

'Yeah, that all makes sense,' she said. 'I can imagine being so kind of, content with Gus that I just slip into a life with him, forgetting that I had a life before.'

'Yeah, you don't want to do that, because apart from anything else, I'm sure one of the things he likes about you is that you do have your own life. Every girl he's ever been out with has been really independent. I think that's what he likes,' said Amy.

'Has he had other girlfriends apart from me?' said Daphne. 'He told me I was the first.'

'Yeah right,' said Amy. 'Should we do yours now?' she asked, turning towards Elli.

'Yeah, okay.'

Amy shuffled the cards and passed them over to Elli. Elli then shuffled and cut the deck and went to turn over the first card. She hesitated.

'What if it says something about dying? Or plane crashes?'

'It so won't say anything about anything like that. They more tell you about who you are, and who you are attracted to, than when you're going to die. I think.'

'Okay,' said Elli. 'Are you sure?'

'Yes. Well, no, I'm not sure, but even if they did show that you were going to die, I probably wouldn't know how to interpret it anyway.'

Elli shuffled the cards, and flipped the top one onto the table.

'The Eight of Cups,' said Amy. 'Hang on.'

'Eight of Cups,' said Elli. 'That sounds a bit boring. You get The Lovers, and I get some bits of crockery.'

'It should be the eight of DD cups,' said Daphne.

Elli laughed. Amy flicked through the book until she came to the right page.

'Hmm, this is interesting. It indicates changes in the sphere of affection. The severing of links with the past which have outlived their relevance. That's good. About time you blew off Ben, I reckon. A turning towards something new and deeper. Can indicate the growth of greater contentment in the future.'

'You know, I haven't thought about Ben for ages.'

Elli turned over the next card. The Two of Cups.

'This symbolises love, emotional affinity, understanding, sympathy, joyous harmony, friendship, co-operation.'

'That sounds quite good,' said Elli.

'Yeah,' said Amy.

Then Elli turned over the card Fortitude. Upside down. Amy raised her eyebrows.

'Okay. I don't know what Fortitude means, but I know that when it's upside down, it means the opposite of whatever it is. I think. Hang on, I'll look it up.'

Amy flicked.

'Here it is. Fortitude represents the individual who, through discipline attains self-control. It shows the positive, outer strength of action.'

'That's good.'

'Yeah, but it's upside down. So it says here you're frightened. You're opening yourself up to defeat because of cowardice. Your failure of nerve could be leading you to a loss of opportunity.'

Elli looked up at Amy, then over at Daphne.

'I wonder what that refers to?' she said.

Daphne dipped her chin, and looked at Elli.

'You think it's to do with Minnow?' Elli asked.

Daphne shrugged.

'Do you think it's saying I should tell Minnow the truth? That if I don't, I'll lose an opportunity? He might be my destiny, but I'll fuck it up if I don't 'fess up?'

'What do you think?' Daphne asked Amy.

'I don't know,' Amy said. 'I'd tell him the truth, but it's up to you. Let's do a few more cards and see what they say.'

The Fool.

'Oh great,' said Elli. 'I'm getting all the good cards.'

Amy smiled.

'No, The Fool is okay. He symbolises new beginnings. See how he's about to step off the cliff? That says he's going to undertake a new journey. He has his bag, which contains memories of what he is leaving behind, memories that will urge him onwards in his search. That's a good card. It says you're going to move forward, despite the risks. It's a very positive card. It probably relates to you going overseas as well, I would imagine. Your trip is the right thing to do.'

'Okay,' said Elli, looking unconvinced. 'With or without the man?'

'Don't know,' said Amy.

Elli turned over her last card.

The Empress.

Amy nodded her head.

'This is another good card. She indicates domestic stability and honesty.'

'Well sure,' said Daphne, 'there's a lot of that happening in your life at the moment.'

'Shut up,' said Elli.

Amy continued.

'She is adept at handling people and reveals a deep understanding of their problems and difficulties. It shows that you are capable of being really upfront. Really honest. Taking consequences on the chin.'

Elli frowned.

'God, I don't know. Maybe I should tell him. But maybe the cards are talking about someone else. Some other guy, not Minnow. Maybe I haven't met the guy yet that the cards are talking about. Maybe I shouldn't tell.'

Amy smiled and poured them all another vodka.

'I don't know,' said Amy.

'I was going to tell him last night,' continued Elli. 'But then that chick Mona came up and kind of put me off. It's not something you can work casually into the conversation. Believe me, I'd love to tell him. We're in the car, kissing, and I'm so busting to say "come up", but I can't because he thinks I've got a kid. And we can't go back to his place because of Lochie. He doesn't think it's right for Lochie to see his dad with a new woman, seeing as his mum only split recently, and that's fair enough, and it even makes me like him more because he's so great about his kid. You know, most guys would think "who gives a shit, I just want to have sex", but Minnow's not like that. He doesn't want to do the wrong thing by Lochie. And because he's such a good dad, makes it even harder for me to say something.'

'Well, maybe you will just have to go overseas and not see him ever again,' said Amy.

'Yeah,' said Elli.

They sat there for a moment. Amy started shuffling the cards, Daphne started rolling another joint. Elli watched them both.

'But I don't want to go overseas and not see him again. I want to keep seeing him. I'd love it for him to come and meet me overseas,' Elli shook her head and shrugged her shoulder. 'I just don't know how to tell him.'

Daphne smiled at Elli and sighed.

'I know it must be hard,' she said. 'I just think the longer you leave it, the worse it's going to get. I mean, if you tell him and he can't handle it, then maybe he wasn't right for you anyway.'

'Yeah, that's true. You're right, I should tell him, and it should be sooner rather than later. I should just bite the bullet, and if it blows up in my face that's just life.'

'When are you seeing him next?'

'Friday night.'

Daphne and Amy both looked at Elli. Elli looked out the window. She looked back at them.

'Alright,' Elli said. 'Okay. I'll tell him Friday night. Happy?'

'Don't do it for us,' said Amy. 'We're not trying to hassle you, it's just that in the end it's going to be better if you tell him and get it out of the way.'

'Yes, I know. I'll tell him Friday.'

Chapter 16

'I hope it works between Minnow and this Elli chick,' Kate said. It was Friday morning. She lay in bed, Lochie snuggled in beside her, watching Ben get dressed. Ben got out a T-shirt and put it on. He pulled on his jeans.

'It feels weird saying "Minnow and Elli", don't you reckon?' she said.

'Why?' Ben asked, as he rifled through his drawer, looking for a jumper.

'You know. Because you used to go out with an Elli. It just sounds weird saying it.'

'I s'pose,' he said, as he pulled a chunky black jumper over his head.

'Don't you think?' she asked.

'No, not really.'

'A bit though.'

Ben sat down on the bed and smiled over at Kate.

'No, not even a bit,' he said.

'Maybe it's just me.'

'Maybe it is.'

He leant forward and started pulling on his RMs.

'Not that I'm jealous of her or anything.'

'Elli?'

'Yeah.'

'You don't need to be jealous of her.'

'Yeah, I know. I'm not.'

'That's good.'

'Who's Elli?' asked Lochie.

'Minnow's new girlfriend,' Ben told him.

'Ben's old girlfriend,' Kate said at the same time.

Ben punched Kate in the arm. Kate giggled.

'Anyway,' Kate said, 'it'll be interesting meeting her tonight.'

'Yeah.'

'Don't you think?'

'Yeah.'

Ben looked over at Kate.

'You're funny,' he said.

'Why?' Kate asked.

'I don't know. You just are.'

'I'm just interested to meet her, that's all. Minnow said he's going to tell her tonight.'

'About the kid thing? Good luck, I reckon.'

'I know. Poor Minnow.'

Kate never imagined she'd ever think 'poor' and 'Minnow' in a sentence together. Except if it was something like 'that poor girl with Minnow'. She remembered a conversation she'd had with Minnow only about six months ago, when he was just back from overseas. He'd been telling her about Amelia, the girl he'd been seeing while he was in England. How Amelia had wanted to get married, and how he couldn't think of anything worse. Marriage was an unnatural state, he'd said, and there was no way he was going to do anything unnatural.

166

'Although some of the things Amelia and I got up to were quite unnatural,' he said with a cocky grin.

'Ugh. That's way too much information,' Kate had said, and told him he should stop selecting his girlfriends on the handbag criteria (that is, how they look hanging on his arm), and instead choose a girl whose personality appealed to him.

'Right,' Minnow had said, leaning forward in his chair and pointing a finger at Kate, 'so name me one ugly guy you've ever gone out with?'

Kate looked at him.

'Excuse me,' she'd said. 'You're saying I only choose my boyfriends on looks? Elliot wasn't that good-looking. Paul wasn't that handsome.'

'That's bullshit. And you could hardly say Ben's in need of a paper bag either.'

'Well, maybe, but I don't choose them because they're good-looking. I choose them because they have good personalities. They just also happen to be good-looking.'

'Elliot didn't.'

'Didn't what?'

'Didn't have a good personality.'

Kate nodded her head and took a sip of her drink.

'Yeah, well. That's true. I just didn't realise until I was pregnant.'

'I read somewhere that Freud reckoned morning sickness was a woman's expression of revulsion for her husband, and an effort to orally abort the child.'

Kate grimaced.

'God, you're scary sometimes.'

'Serious. I think that was the same book which also mentioned that 10,000 years ago the average length of a union was only four years.'

'Four years would be some kind of record for you, wouldn't it?'

'Yeah, I'm no Neanderthal.'

But that was then. This is now. Now Minnow was hooked. This new chick Elli had caught him, and the only problem was the tangled web he'd weaved, which was now threatening to bring him to a sticky end.

'You know,' Minnow had told Kate yesterday, 'I really want to do the right thing by her. I'm not even slightly interested in being with other girls.'

'It's early-days yet.'

'No, seriously. You've gotta meet her. You'd really like her.'

'Minnow,' Kate said, 'I've gotta be straight with you. I don't want to meet her yet. Not while she still thinks you've got a kid. It would be too awkward. What if she asked me about Lochie? What if she asked me what kind of dad you are? I couldn't lie to her. Once you've told her, I'd love to meet her. But until then, I just think it's best left.'

Minnow had told Kate he was going to tell Elli. Tonight. He said he wanted Kate, Ben, and Doug there at the beginning, he wanted them to meet her, and then when they left to go to The Espy, he was going to tell her.

'Wouldn't it be better for us to meet her after you've told her?' asked Kate. 'That way, if she's cool with it we can get to know her, and if she spins out and tells you to fuck off, we don't have to waste our time making small talk with someone who's not going to be around for long.'

Minnow had leaned forward, resting his arms on his knees, examining the ground.

'I suppose,' he said quietly, 'I just want you to meet her because if it doesn't work out, if she does tell me to fuck off,

I just want you to see that she really was fantastic. That I wasn't just making it up. That's all.'

Kate had looked at the top of Minnow's head. He was always so cocky. Such a lad. So couldn't-give-a-shit. She'd never seen him look humble. Never. Never, ever, ever. She had put her arm around his shoulders. She had pursed her lips and then sighed.

'Okay, we'll come,' she'd said. 'Besides, I'm sure once you tell her, she'll be fine with it.'

Minnow continued watching the ground. Kate hugged his strangely humble shoulders.

'I'm busting to meet her,' she said. 'It'll be good. And honestly, I'm sure once you tell her she'll be fine. She might be a bit annoyed, but once she gets used to the idea, she'll be fine with it. I'm sure.'

Not.

Chapter 17

Elli had no intention of taking Jacinta with her tonight. She didn't hang out with Jacinta, she didn't particularly like Jacinta, she certainly didn't want to go and meet Minnow's friends for the first time with Jacinta in tow. But after what had happened this afternoon, there didn't seem to be a whole lot of other options available.

Elli had finished work Friday afternoon and was sitting up at the counter talking to Tristan, sipping a green tea. Jacinta was sitting beside them, silently dipping sticks into honey for customers who liked to sweeten their tea. Elli always enjoyed doing the honey, it was relaxing. There was a tray of sticks, small and a bit nobbly, with wire twisted delicately around each end. You'd pick up a stick, dip one end into a pot of honey — which Dave and Tristan brought back especially from a farm near their holiday house — and then you'd twirl the stick rhythmically, bringing it slowly out of the honey, twirling, twirling, until the honey crystallised.

'First up,' Elli was telling Tristan, 'I'm going to Thailand. I'll stay there for a couple of weeks, then on to Kathmandu where I want to do a trek. Next, I fly in to London, and I'm going to stay with these friends of mine for a bit.'

'That'll be good. Do they work over there?'

'Yeah. He's a lawyer, and she's a florist. They're gorgeous, you'd really like them. Then after London, I'm going to Italy. I've got some rellies that I can bunk down with there, and I'd like to try and get work so I can hang out there for a few months.'

'But what about your man of the moment? What are you going to do about him? You don't want to have a boyfriend while you're travelling around. Especially not with all those handsome Italian men.'

'Yeah, I know. I'm not sure what's going to happen there. It's all a bit complicated and I still haven't told him about the Daphne thing.'

Elli noticed that Jacinta looked up at her sharply when she mentioned Daphne's name.

'What?' she asked Jacinta.

'No, nothing,' Jacinta replied.

'Anyway,' said Elli, turning back to Tristan, 'he said he wants to come and meet me over there.'

'In Italy?'

'Wherever. He's said he'd even consider tossing in his job to come with me.'

'Omigod. That's serious.'

'I know. I'd love it if he did, but it's all a bit too complicated. One of the reasons I thought it would be quite good to go overseas was so that I didn't have to confront all these things.'

'It's a tangled web we weave,' said Tristan.

'Ain't that the truth,' said Elli.

The phone rang and Tristan picked it up.

'The Tea House. How may I help you?'

He listened for a moment.

'Speak of the devil,' he said, and handed the phone over to Elli.

'Hello?' she said.

'Hi, it's me,' said Minnow. 'I was just ringing to make sure you're still up for tonight.'

Elli smiled to herself. She was really looking forward to meeting his friends. She was really looking forward to seeing him. She was really looking forward to sitting in his car and kissing him. She wasn't really looking forward to telling him the kid thing was bullshit.

'Yeah, you bet.'

'Good. Afterwards, we might go to The Espy. Kate's boyfriend's band is playing.'

'Oh. Okay.'

Elli didn't know Doug played in a band.

'Are you sure you don't want me to come and pick you up?' Minnow asked.

'No, honestly, I'm fine. I'll meet you there. It's a bit easier for me.'

'I'm happy to.'

'I know you are.'

'Elli, when am I going to meet Daphne?' Minnow asked. 'You never let me pick you up. You never let me drop you home. I know we've only been seeing each other for a few weeks, and you think it's too soon for Daphne, but . . .'

'Listen Minnow, can we talk about this later? I'm at work at the moment. We can discuss it tonight if you want. Okay?'

She looked over at Jacinta, who was standing, frozen and furious, stick mid-dip, focusing on Elli. Elli winced.

'I've gotta go. I'll see you at eight,' Elli said and hung up the phone.

Jacinta slammed the stick she'd been dipping on the counter, honey globbing in a puddle, and glared at Elli. Elli frowned.

'Minnow?' Jacinta said.

'Excuse me?' said Elli.

'You're going out with Minnow?' Jacinta said, sarcasm globbing in a puddle on the counter next to the honey stick.

'Yes,' Elli enunciated clearly, with a double 's' on the end. 'Do you have a problem with that?'

'You're fucking Minnow, are you?'

Elli pulled her head away from Jacinta, as if being close to her was distasteful.

'Well, actually, no, I'm not "fucking" him, if it's any of your business, but yes, we are seeing each other. Why? Did you used to go out with him or something?'

Jacinta laughed, but it wasn't a pleasant sound. Not a tinkle like when Daphne laughed. Or a snort like Amy did sometimes, which always cracked them all up. This was a laugh which scraped its way out of Jacinta's throat, scratching its way up to be spat into Elli's face.

'No, I didn't "used to go out with him". I'm still going out with him. We've been together for about a month and a half.' Jacinta paused and looked at Elli. 'I am fucking him.'

Elli's shoulders dropped.

'Minnow?'

'Yes,' said Jacinta, folding her arms in front of her and raising her chin in a challenge to Elli.

'Are you sure it's the same one?' Elli asked.

Jacinta laughed again. That same spiteful sound.

'How many Minnow's do you think there are?'

'Is your one blond, tall and slim?' asked Elli.

'Yes.'

'And he lives in Elwood?'

'Yes.'

'And he's friends with Doug and Kate?'

'Yes.'

Jacinta's arms were still folded, the chin still cocked like a pistol.

'But he told me he wasn't seeing anyone else,' said Elli. 'He said I was the only one.'

Jacinta shrugged a shoulder. 'Well, you're not,' she said.

Elli felt limp. She didn't feel angry. She didn't feel upset. She just felt limp. She felt like her whole body was a down-turned mouth. She had really trusted Minnow. She couldn't believe that he was seeing Jacinta. He had said that when he wasn't with Elli, he was just with mates. Well, now it seemed that wasn't quite the truth.

'Have you met Lochie?' Elli asked.

Jacinta looked at Elli and cocked her chin higher.

'Yes, of course I have,' she said.

So that's why Minnow didn't want her to meet Lochie. It would be too confusing for him. Lochie knew Jacinta. If his dad brought home Elli as well, Lochie wouldn't know what was going on. All that crap about not wanting Lochie to meet a new woman too soon after his mum had left was bullshit. He was fucking Jacinta, she was obviously staying over at his place on the nights when he wasn't with Elli.

'What a fucking arsehole,' Elli said, brushing her hair off her face, and rubbing her eyes. 'Have you met like, Kate and Doug and all those guys?'

Jacinta dropped her chin a bit, before lifting it up in a challenge once more.

'I haven't actually met them yet, but I know who they are. Minnow said he wants me to meet them soon.'

Elli continued rubbing her eyes, as if trying to get her life back into focus.

'I can't believe this,' she said. 'I cannot believe he's seeing both of us.'

She looked up at Jacinta.

'Well,' Elli said, raising her eyebrows, 'why don't you come and meet them with me? Tonight? We're meeting at Crush at eight o'clock. The more the merrier, I always say. And it'll be interesting to see what Minnow has to say when we both show up. Together.'

'Um,' Jacinta faltered, 'I'm not sure.'

Elli looked back at Jacinta. The challenge wasn't there any more, it was just Jacinta, alone.

'What?' Elli said. 'You're sleeping with Minnow, he's seeing me as well, and you don't want to confront him? I don't get it. Are you really seeing him, or are you just bull-shitting me?'

Jacinta pulled her arms back into position. The challenge was back on. Jacinta scoffed at Elli.

'Yeah, I'm bullshitting you. I've got nothing better in my life to do than to pretend I'm seeing the same guy you are. As if. Iqbal,' Jacinta said, looking carefully at Elli to see if she recognised the phrase. Yep, Elli knew it. She knew nothing about cricket, but she knew about Asif Iqbal, the Pakistani cricket player.

'Yeah, I'll come along,' said Jacinta. 'What time was it again?'

'We're meeting at eight. We can meet outside just before if you want.'

'Yeah. I will. I'll see you there.'

And Jacinta walked off, not even bothering to pick up the

honey stick that had crystallised onto the surface of the counter.

Elli looked over at Tristan, who couldn't seem to find any words that were appropriate. He put his arm around her and gave her a squeeze. Elli wasn't looking forward to the night anymore. Not half as much as she had been.

Chapter 18

Elli felt ugly. Dog ugly. Pig dog ugly. Fugly. Fucking ugly. She'd done her best. Green gingham bra and matching G-string. Red top and green pants, with her Chinese slippers. So far it wasn't working. She still felt lacklustre. Dull. Unattractive. Awful.

As far as Elli was concerned, there were three kinds of days in a week: Hip hop happy days where she could put on any old thing, be any old place and feel fantabulous. They were the days when she was dancing all the time, even if she wasn't moving a muscle. Then there were shitful days. Pretty self-explanatory, those ones. If she made a phone call, the person wasn't there. If she blow-dried her hair, it went skewiff. If it was busy at work, she had all the tables of two women, 'Just an entrée for me, thanks,' with the corresponding pathetic tip. And finally, there were invisible days. These were the worst days of all. At least on shitful days, people could see you. People talked to you. People recognised you. But on invisible days, it was the strangest thing. It was like no one could see you. For example, there was that time, about six months ago, just after she and Ben had split up. To say she'd been feeling lacklustre is to totally undersell how absolutely shithouse she had felt. Amy knew Elli was in dire need of cheering up, so she'd arranged for Elli to meet Amy, Hugh, and Daphne down at The Prince for a drink, and then they were going to go out for dinner somewhere. It was going to be fun, Amy had said. It'll make you feel heaps better, she'd said. It's just what you need, she'd said. So Elli sat at The Prince, waiting for her friends to arrive, sitting there, at a table, on her own, waiting, waiting, waiting, watching all the other people sitting at tables with their friends, laughing, having a good time, while she sat at a table on her own, feeling less good every minute that dragged by, watching out carefully for her friends, but not seeing anyone. Eventually she'd gone home. It would certainly rank up there as one of the memorably bad nights of her life.

The next morning, Daphne had come into the kitchen to find Elli sitting at the table, toast uneaten on her plate. Toast with Vegemite, of course, not mahrm-ah-layd.

'What happened to you?' Daphne had asked.

'I was there,' said Elli through a tight, pissed off mouth. So tight was her mouth, in fact, she could only barely slot her toast through it.

'You were at The Prince?'

'Yes,' said Elli, through slot-mouth, pulled tight.

'Well, that's weird,' said Daphne, 'because we walked around heaps of times, but couldn't find you. We thought maybe you'd had to work a double. Where were you sitting?'

'At the corner table, near the window.'

'I don't know. Maybe because it was a bit crowded we couldn't see you, but we seriously looked at every table.'

And that was when Elli realised she had invisible days. She figured it was kind of like a time-dimension-reality thing, or something. Like, maybe she was invisible because she went into an entirely different zone altogether. Maybe she was so depressed on certain occasions, that her spirit became wafer-thin, and accidently vanished through one of those *Lion, The Witch and The Wardrobe* portal things, and it was only once she felt a bit more pumped that she came back into reality. In fact, she'd expanded her theory of invisible days to include invisible cars. Maybe cars accidentally sometimes went through these time dimension things, and then suddenly reappeared on the streets. That would account for people getting knocked over. Obviously, if the car was there you wouldn't step off the footpath in front of it — you'd stay on the footpath until it had passed. But people who were knocked over always said, 'I never even saw it until it was on top of me.' When you think about it, it makes sense, the sixth dimension thing Elli had figured out. And if it was on 'The X Files' you wouldn't think it was strange. You'd think it sounded perfectly normal, in fact.

Elli looked at herself in the mirror and tried to decide. Was she having a shitful day? Or an invisible day? Was it merely bad, or was it totally, sixth dimensionally depressing? So depressing that she'd gone into another zone entirely, and was only a faint outline of herself? She looked at herself care-fully. Watched her eyes. Watched her mouth. Looked at her clothes. Into her eyes. She breathed slowly, like she had seen Daphne do when she was meditating. She stopped breathing. Everything was still. She felt calm. She realised that she cer-tainly didn't feel a zoned-out depression. That was a good thing. That had to be a positive, she figured. She took another deep breath, exhaled, and stopped breathing again. Still. Calm.

Actually, she realised that she didn't even feel particularly shitful. She felt wired. She felt completely zinged. She felt a rush, her arms felt a bit shaky. She held her hand out in front of her face. It was trembling a bit. But she didn't feel delicate. Not fragile, or faint. She felt a charge. Electricity, or something. Her hand was shaking because she was hyper-there, not because she was going to pass out. That had to be a good thing. Like, she didn't feel hip hop happy, that would certainly be overstating things, but she didn't feel sooo bad.

She looked at herself in the mirror again. Actually, she decided, she didn't look pig dog ugly at all. She would almost say she looked okay. Not as good as she would have liked to have looked when she was meeting Minnow's friends for the first time, but not too bad. She studied herself in the mirror. Normally she liked these clothes. Normally when she put on this top with these pants, she liked the way she looked. She just had to remember that. She had to remember that if she was feeling happy, she would think she looked good. But tonight, because she was feeling a bit uncertain, she was also uncertain how she looked. On the one hand, she was thinking of changing her outfit, and on the other hand, thinking she'd persevere. She decided to go with the other hand and postpone judgment for a bit longer. It was like when she was doing a canvas at art school. You really couldn't make an assessment until the last bit had been painted. That might just be the finishing touch needed to bring it all together. She started blow-drying her hair.

Minnow was seeing Jacinta. He was sleeping with her. Jacinta had met Lochie. She'd been seeing Minnow for over a month. He'd been with her even when he'd come into The Tea House that night. Maybe he'd come into The Tea House to see Jacinta, but she wasn't working. Elli should have asked Jacinta if she knew Mona. She probably did. Minnow had told Elli that he hadn't been with anyone since he'd met up with her again that night at The Tea House. She'd believed him. He'd seemed so honest. He'd looked her in the eye and said, 'I haven't been with anyone since I met you.' Straight out. She couldn't believe he could just look at her and lie like that.

'I don't think you can really get on your high horse about him lying to you,' Daphne had pointed out, as Elli blow-dried her hair.

'That's completely different.'

'Really?'

'Come on. I mean, I know I totally told a lie, but that was the first time I met him, and I didn't know him, and it was more of a test than a lie, really, if you think about it. But since we've started seeing each other, I haven't once looked him in the face and told him about my kid.'

Daphne looked at Elli and raised an eyebrow.

'I haven't,' Elli insisted, straightening sections of her hair carefully. 'Whenever he asks about my kid I just change the subject really quickly. I mean, admittedly I say "she's good" or something like that, but I never look him straight in the eye when I say it. I always look away. But he's looked me straight in the face and told me that he wasn't seeing anyone else. He said he hasn't even so much as called another girl since we started seeing each other.'

'Well, maybe there's a mistake. Maybe Jacinta's lying. Maybe she's not really seeing him, maybe she just slept with him a couple of times and has made it out to be more than it is. I mean, you've only been seeing Minnow for a few weeks. Maybe he was with her in the early stages. And now she's made it into a bigger deal than it really was. In fact, maybe she knows she doesn't really mean anything to him and she's just deliberately trying to hurt him. Through you.'

'I don't think so. I mean, I wouldn't say we're best friends, but we're certainly not enemies. She wouldn't deliberately try to hurt me.' Elli turned off the hair dryer and arranged her hair to look like she'd made zero effort.

'Yes, but I'm saying she mightn't be doing it to hurt you,' said Daphne. 'She might be doing it to hurt him. She might be angry that he slept with her a few times and it meant nothing, so now she's making it into something more to get back at him. Do you know what I mean?'

'Yeah.' Elli started rifling through her makeup basket. She sucked her cheeks in and bronzed up her 'apples'. 'I don't know,' said Elli. 'Maybe. Or maybe she really is seeing him, you know, going out with him, and he's just stringing the two of us along. And she's met Lochie, remember?'

'Yeah, that's true.'

Daphne shook her head and looked down at her nails, pushing down a couple of untidy cuticles. Bit a stubborn one off. She looked back up at Elli.

'So you're going to meet her at Crush, and then do the big confrontation thing with Minnow?'

'Yep.'

'Are you sure that's a good idea?'

Elli got out her eyeliner and started linering her eyes.

'Yes. Absolutely. I mean, if he really is seeing both of us, then he deserves it.'

'But what if he's not seeing both of you? What if he's really seeing just you, and Jacinta has made it out to be more than it really is? Then you might feel like a bit of an idiot. And he might feel pissed off. And then if you're going to tell him about not really having a kid, then it's going to make it worse.'

184

Mascara.

'But I'm not going to tell him about not having a kid.'

'I thought you were.'

'Well, I was, but that's all changed now. If he's seeing someone else, then it was good that I lied and set up a bit of a barrier. I mean, if he's seeing her as well as me, then it's good that I said I had a kid because at least it meant I didn't sleep with him. At least he didn't get that out of me.'

Lipliner.

'But what if he's not seeing her? You keep assuming that he is, but what if he's not?'

Elli stopped outlining her lips. She looked at Daphne thoughtfully.

Daphne continued.

'Why don't you go by yourself, and talk to him on your own? Ask him if he's seeing Jacinta. See what he says. I just don't know if I'd trust Jacinta. Besides,' said Daphne, 'didn't you say she was seeing some rich guy? If she really is seeing Minnow, it sounds like he's just one of a number. Maybe she just collects men and it doesn't really mean anything.'

Elli pursed her lips.

'That's true. I'd forgotten about that guy. Although she hasn't mentioned him for a while. Maybe she's not seeing him anymore.'

Red, red, red lipstick.

'I just think if you both show up together, it's like you're asking for a fight.'

'Do you think?'

'Definitely. If I was you I'd go on my own. Ring Jacinta. Tell her not to come.'

'I don't have her number.'

'Ring work and get it. Just go on your own. You and Minnow have enough shit to sort out, without Jacinta coming along.'

'Yeah, that's true.'

She plucked a few stray eyebrow hairs.

'Go on,' said Daphne, 'you look great. Ring work. If you ring her too late, she might have left already.'

Elli sighed.

'I just don't know.'

Daphne shrugged her shoulders.

'Well, you don't have to. It's up to you.'

But she said it in that bored voice which really meant the opposite. Like she was trying to sound not involved, like she didn't care, like it was up to Elli, but really, if Elli didn't do what she suggested it would be foolish. Elli rang work. Jacinta wasn't there but Philby gave her Jacinta's home number. When Elli rang her home, she just got the answering machine. She hung up.

'You don't want to leave a message?' Daphne asked.

'I don't know,' said Elli. 'In some ways, I think it might be quite good if Jacinta comes along. I mean, she definitely knows him. She's met his kid. She knows his friends. She even said that "Iqbal" thing that he says. I mean, she's not lying about knowing him. And if he is seeing her as well as me, I'd like to know. I don't want him to be able to bullshit me and say she's nothing, or he's not with her, or whatever he might say. I want her there, and then he has to deal with it. With both of us. I mean, I was thinking before all this happened that I'd tell him about not having a kid. I don't want to go and say all that if he's some arsehole. And if he's seeing me and Jacinta, who knows who else he's seeing? He could have a full-on harem going, for all I know.'

Daphne nodded.

'Yeah, I suppose you'll get it all out in the open, that's for sure,' she said.

'If he's not seeing Jacinta, if she's just made it up, then it'll just be embarrassing for her. I'll know straightaway, just by his face, whether he's stringing us both along or not.'

'You know,' said Daphne, 'it's weird that he never asked you about her. I mean, he knows you both work at The Tea House, surely he would have mentioned her to you? Or you to her.'

Elli thought for a minute.

'Yeah, that's true. But she definitely knows him. She knows his friends. There can't be two Minnows with the same friends, the same kid, and the same sayings.'

'No.'

Elli had a sneaky idea.

'Why don't you come with me?' she asked. 'For moral support?'

'No,' said Daphne. 'I'd walk in, and you'd say "this is Daphne" and Minnow would say "isn't she supposed to be about three feet shorter?" and you'd be sprung badly. Then it would go from being about him lying, to being about you lying.'

Elli put her hand on Daphne's arm.

'You know, that's perfect.'

'What? No.'

'Go on. This is the perfect way to tell him.'

'No way.'

'Please?'

'Forget it.'

'Pretty please?'

'Don't even bother.'

So now Elli was driving to meet Minnow and his friends at Crush, but she was going to be walking in with Jacinta, and it all seemed like a really bad idea. She looked at the clock on the dash. Seven forty-five. Maybe if she got there before eight, she could walk in and Jacinta could walk in later. Would that be mean? Did Elli really care? She decided to let fate decide. If Jacinta wasn't out the front when she arrived, she'd go in without her.

Minnow felt pumped. He'd decided to tell Elli the truth. Tonight. And it felt good. He was surprised at how good he felt. He felt fucking great. He had it all worked out. They'd have dinner with Doug, Kate and Ben, then, instead of going to The Espy with those guys, he'd say to Elli, 'Do you want to have one more drink here before we go to watch Ben play? I want to tell you something.'

Then he'd grab them both a drink and sit back down with her and he'd tell her. He'd tell her straight out. He'd start with the first night he met her. Tell her that he thought she was a real babe, but the fact that she had a kid spun him out.

'But now,' he'd say, 'I'm okay with you having a kid. I really dig you, and I think it's cool that you've got a kid. And I'm really ready to meet Daphne. I know you said you don't think it's right for Daphne to meet a guy unless it's serious, but I gotta tell you, I'm really serious about you. I've never felt like this about anyone in my life.'

Maybe that was a bit too sucky. That bit about 'never felt like this about anyone before'. Best to leave it at 'I'm really serious about you.' And then he'd tell her that when he went for the job at 625 FM, he'd decided he didn't really want it. He'd rather work part-time. Didn't want the full-on career just yet. So he'd pretended that he had a kid. He'd say he knew it was the wrong thing to do. A low blow. But it had just kind of come out, and once he'd said it and they said he could have the reduced hours, it seemed too easy. And then he'd say it had all blown out of proportion, that he'd never intended for her to hear the thing about him having a kid; it was just that Tristan had said it (or Dave, or Philby, or whoever), and he'd say he could understand if she was really mad with him. And then he'd ask her to please, please, please, forgive him, and give him a chance to start afresh with her. No lies.

He felt great.

Jacinta felt ditched already. And she was pretty pissed off about it.

She knew, just knew for a fact, that Minnow would choose Elli over her. Jacinta screwed her face up in the mirror, mimicking Minnow telling her: 'But Elli's so cute. Look at her. So adorable. Cute as a button.' And then Jacinta would ask him how cute he thought it was that Elli was a cold, calculating, blackmailing criminal. 'How cute do you think that is?' she'd ask Minnow.

Jacinta had had a shit week and a half. The letter from Elli had started it. Steven had been a complete prick on the phone to her, and then on Monday night when they'd caught up. Arsehole. Complete fucking arsehole. He obviously still thought Jacinta might be in on the scam, and he kept making these comments about how 'That was all the money they'd get out of him', and how 'It would be unwise to ask for more', as if Jacinta would pass the message on to Elli for him.

But he told her not to mention it to Elli.

'I forbid you to say anything to her,' he'd said.

189

Forbid. Right. Like he was her fucking father or some-thing. And they'd sat at Aesop's, eating this beautiful food and drinking this yummy wine, and it all tasted sour to her. It didn't taste yum. It didn't taste good. It was tainted. Every other night they'd been out together, at least he was reason-ably interesting to listen to, banging on about himself and his deals, and this and that. But the Monday after the letter crap? He'd just carried on about extortion the whole night. How people are always out to get him. How he has to watch his back all the time. Told her that they all hated it when the Top 100 List came out each year.

'All the lowlife scum come out and start trying to juice you for some cash,' he'd said. 'When I'm trying to do deals, they think they can screw me.'

'Well, you shouldn't have paid,' Jacinta had said. It seemed reasonable. But he'd just looked at her as if she was some kind of double-crossing Butch Cassidy and told her that it wasn't worth it not to pay. It wasn't so much the money in fact, but the principle that irked him more than anything else.

'The principle?' she'd felt like saying. 'Don't pretend you've got principles.'

But she didn't say that. She had just sat there waiting for the evening to finish, but not wanting it to finish because once it finished she was going to have to have sex with him, and if the food at Aesop's didn't taste as good as it usually did, the thought of sex with him later that night left a real bad taste in her mouth.

The next day, the first thing she'd done was go to the bank to see how much money she had, and if she could get a loan to move into a flat of her own. But the scary thing was, she wasn't sure if she could afford to live on her own — afford the rent and the bills. And the car. She'd need to get a new car. She wished she'd taken advantage of Steven more, saved up a gazillion dollars. But her bank account didn't look that healthy. It didn't look real sick, but it didn't look majorly fabulous either. She had enough to pay the bond and a month's rent, but that was about it.

So she'd started looking at flats, but because she was living at Steven's place, she couldn't give him as a reference to new landlords, and she'd applied for about seven flats and been knocked back every time. She had been starting to feel really trapped, and wasn't sure what she was going to do on the Steven front. She wanted to move, but it seemed she was being blocked at every turn.

The only thing that had made the past couple of weeks bearable was Minnow. And now she found out that he was seeing Elli as well. But not sleeping with her. What did that mean? Was Elli some born again virgin who refused to sleep with a guy before she was married? She sure didn't look it. Or maybe Minnow didn't want to sleep with her, because he was sleeping with Jacinta? Which would mean he liked Jacinta more than he liked Elli. But maybe he liked Elli more than Jacinta, and that's why he hadn't slept with her. Maybe he respected Elli, and he didn't respect Jacinta? Of all the things about Elli being with Minnow, the fact that she wasn't sleeping with him bothered Jacinta the most.

Jacinta got into the shower. If she was going to be dumped tonight, she was going to make sure she looked fucking fantastic. And she was going to make sure she smelt absolutely divine. And her clothes were going to be just so. She was going to walk into Crush with Elli, and every guy was going to look at her, not Elli. If she was going to be dumped, she was going to make certain she didn't look the part.

She got out of the shower and assessed herself in the mirror. She looked good. But you know, even without her clothes on, her hair wet, no makeup, she still looked like a mistress. What was it about her that said mistress? Why did no guy want to have her as his numero uno?

The phone rang. She didn't answer it. If it was Steven, she wasn't in the mood to talk to him. And if it was Minnow . . . actually, if it was Minnow she'd love to talk to him. She had really felt like they had something happening, she'd really believed him when he said he was into her. Although now she thought about it, she should have been suspicious that he didn't want to introduce her to any of his friends. That was a sure sign. He didn't want her to meet any of them because he was saving them for Elli.

And who was Lochie? He was obviously someone quite important to Minnow, because he'd been one of the first people Elli had asked about. But Minnow had never mentioned Lochie to her. He'd talked about Doug and Kate, she'd known those names when Elli mentioned them, but she didn't know who Lochie was. Maybe he was some retarded brother, like in *Rain Man*? Or maybe he was some friend who was a junkie, who Minnow looked after sometimes. Could be anyone.

She listened to the beep, beep, beep, of the answering machine. She hated it when people didn't leave a message. That's what answering machines are for. To leave a message. She even spelt it out at the beginning of each call, 'Hi, you've called Jacinta. I can't get to the phone right now, so, leave a message.' How hard could it be? If someone rang to speak to her, surely they could leave a fucking message if she didn't answer the phone. It wasn't that hard. If they went to the trouble of ringing her, surely they could go that one step further and actually leave a message to let her know who called.

She wished she hadn't heard Elli speaking to Minnow that afternoon. She recalled a few times Tristan or Dave had answered the phone and handed it to Elli saying 'lover boy' or 'the man', but she'd never heard Elli say his name before. She hadn't realised that Elli's 'lover boy' was also hers. It just didn't seem fair.

She went to her wardrobe. The outfit was very important. She had to look great, but not look like she was trying to look great. She had to look like she just happened to look this good without putting in much effort. It was a fine tightrope. One step too far this way, and she'd plunge into the vast wasteland of 'too casual, not enough effort'. One step the other side, and she'd fall into the 'too try-hard' category. Boys had no idea how hard it was for girls to get dressed for a date. She decided on her black leather pants, black boots, cream turtleneck, and black scarf. Hair down. She always wore her hair down. Concealer, foundation, blusher, eye shadow, eyeliner, mascara, eyebrow pencil, lip liner, lipstick.

She looked at her watch. Seven-thirty. It was going to take her 15 minutes to get there. She'd better leave now. She wanted to get there a bit before eight. Be there before Elli got there.

Chapter 19

Crush, Friday night, 7:55. Don't expect to just nick up to the bar, grab a drink, and sit back down. Other nights of the week, sure. Friday nights, no. Bar too crowded. People too many. Friday nights you'll hear these predictable snippets from fairly early on.

'No wonder they call it Crush.'

'You know what they say — Crush by name, Crush by nature.'

'A Crush by any other name would be as tight.'

And other corn. Not necessarily pick-up lines, although you'd notice they're not said to the ugly girls standing at the bar. The ugly girls are given a glance, a smile, and then the head swivels to see what's on the other side.

Ben was up at the bar getting drinks, so Kate, Minnow and Doug didn't expect to see him for a fairly long while. Minnow, Kate and Doug were chatting. Actually, Kate and Doug were chatting, Minnow was sitting there, smiling, nodding in all the right spots, but he couldn't tell you what they were talking about. Just the usual crap he supposed. But he wasn't listening to it. He was inside his own head, rehearsing over and over how the night would go. He'd introduce Elli to Kate, Doug, and Ben. He'd get Elli a drink and she'd stay at the table, chatting to his friends. Hopefully, she wouldn't ask anything about Lochie, because he knew Kate well enough to know she wouldn't lie for him. She might avoid the question, but if she was asked something straight out by Elli, she'd tell the truth. She couldn't help it. She was Catholic. Hopefully it wouldn't come up. Then he'd sit back down with her and watch her talking to his friends. Watch that sexy mouth of hers making words, making conversation. They'd order something for dinner. Eat. Ben had to leave around ten to set up for tonight, Kate and Doug would probably leave a bit after that. They'd ask if he and Elli were coming.

'No,' Minnow would say, 'we'll meet you there.'

Then he would tell Elli all about Lochie. He knew she'd be pissed off. He expected that. But he'd tell her he wanted to talk more. Explain how he felt about her. Tell her how keen he was to meet her daughter.

Afterwards, they'd go to The Espy, see Ben's band playing. Have a good night. And then, if she wanted, she could come back to his place. Or go back to her place. And they'd lie together. But he wouldn't have sex with her. Unless he absolutely, positively, had to. Unless she forced him. But he would rather wait a bit longer. Wait until she completely trusted him. Wait until she had come to terms with his lie.

He felt like a virgin. He felt like a girl. He felt an erection blooming. Whenever he thought of Elli, he'd get a schwing. It was like he was programmed. His dad had told him once about a patient he had who was on chemotherapy. Every time his dad saw this patient, he had to give her these really heavy-duty drugs and she'd end up vomiting. Then, one time, after she'd finished treatment and was fine, his dad saw her at the airport and went up to say hello. And she'd vomited. Right there. Without any drugs or anything. Just from seeing him, she'd done a chuck. It was a response mechanism, Minnow's dad had said. Just like the response mechanism Minnow associated with Elli. A stiffie. A bit of general fluffing up every time he thought of her. He couldn't help it. Elli. Schwing. Elli. Schwing. See? Automatic.

'Hi, Minnow.'

Minnow looked up and saw Elli standing there. Elli and some other girl.

Elli had had trouble finding a car park. Ormond Road was getting out of control. It was really irritating. When she'd first moved into Elwood, Ormond Road had been a park-outside-the-shop-you're-going-into-type street. But now it was ridiculously popular, so on a Friday night there was no way you could park anywhere near the place you wanted to go to. She had eventually found a park about halfway down Beach Avenue, and then had to walk all the way back to Ormond Road in her Chinese slippers, which were definitely not made by Nike, which was a shame, because she wanted to get to Crush as quickly as possible. She wanted to run. She wanted to be there before Jacinta got there. She wanted to go in, and not have the confrontation with Minnow, and if Jacinta came in afterwards and found them, then she could make the hysterical scene by herself and Elli would just sit back and watch what happened. See if Jacinta really was telling the truth about dating Minnow. Sleeping with him.

Because the more Elli thought about it, the more she thought it was crap. Minnow — her Minnow — wouldn't go for someone like Jacinta. If he liked Elli, then Jacinta certainly wasn't his type. Jacinta was so different from Elli. She was so obvious. So obviously available. Shimmying her arse all over work. Sure, she was pretty. Sure, she wore expensive clothes. But expensive didn't necessarily mean nice. Her clothes were more come-fuck-me than anything else. Like that snakeskin coat she sometimes wore to work. Or the knee-high boots with the shorty-shorts. There was a fine line between groovy and tarty, and Jacinta lunged enthusiastically over that line continually. And Minnow had never mentioned Jacinta to Elli. That was definitely strange. If he really was seeing her, then surely he'd have to say something to Elli, seeing as they worked together.

Maybe Jacinta was a stalker. Maybe she'd met Minnow briefly one night, and now she was following him. Getting to know all about him that way. Elli remembered that Minnow said he thought Mona was a bit of a bunny boiler, that he often got phone calls where noone would speak, had the feeling of someone watching through his windows occasionally. Maybe it wasn't Mona. Maybe it was Jacinta. That made more sense than anything. Jacinta was stalking Minnow. She had to be. There was no other answer. That's why Minnow had never mentioned her.

Elli came around the corner into Ormond Road. Shit. Jacinta was already there, sitting outside Crush, waiting. Like some kind of spider. That's what she reminded Elli of. A spider. Long, thin, and black. Even though she was blonde. She had a blackness to her that all those bottles of peroxide couldn't cover. She looked like a stalker.

'Are you ready?' asked Jacinta.

'No,' Elli wanted to say. 'Let's not,' was the first thing that sprang to mind. 'We'll sort it out later,' was the next option.

'Let's not do this.' But she didn't say any of it. She looked at Jacinta, took a deep breath, and said, 'Yep. Let's go.'

They walked into Crush. It was hot. Crowded. There must have been forty people standing at the bar, waiting to be served. Five bartenders. A bit like Ormond Road itself — forty cars, five car spaces. Elli saw Jacinta craning her head left, right, forward, glancing back. Elli bit her lip and also started looking at people's faces, studying groups at tables, excuse-me-excuse-me-ing through the crowd. One guy blocked her path and just looked down at her, didn't move, smiled. Elli didn't smile back. Her eyes circumnavigated him, looking for Minnow, trying to find where he was, hoping he might not even be here so the whole awful business could be avoided.

If Jacinta was a stalker, Elli was leading her straight to Minnow. And if Jacinta really was seeing Minnow, but it was only some kind of casual nothing, then it was going to be really awkward. And if she was really seeing Minnow full-on as a girlfriend, it was going to be really, really, awkward. Elli wished she hadn't suggested Jacinta come along. It suddenly seemed like a really bad idea. Really bad.

And then she saw him. Sitting at a table with a guy and a girl. The guy looked similar to him. Same blondy-brown hair, cut shortish. Broad shoulders. A handsome face. They could be brothers. Elli figured it must be Doug. And there was a girl with her back to Elli. Straight black hair. That must be Kate.

Elli went over and stood behind Minnow. Looked down at him carefully to see his reaction when he saw Jacinta. Said 'Hi.' Minnow looked up at Elli and smiled, his eyes, mouth, even his ears tilted happily at her. He looked over at Jacinta but didn't seem to recognise her. He frowned slightly for a moment, but then his face came back to Elli's and settled on her. He stood up, kissed her on the mouth. Elli could have sung, screamed, yelled, pounded the floor with her feet. He didn't know Jacinta. She could see by his face, by the way he held her, by the way he kissed her, that it was a big fat Iqbal, him knowing Jacinta.

He looked over at Jacinta, waiting to be introduced.

Elli said: 'This is Jacinta. Have you guys met?'

But when she looked at Jacinta, Jacinta wasn't looking at Minnow. She was looking at the guy Elli presumed was Doug. Jacinta hadn't even noticed Minnow. Elli looked down at Doug. He was watching Jacinta, but he didn't seem that pleased to see her. Actually, he looked like he had something stuck in his throat. He looked like he was about to gag.

This was not the plan. This was not how it was meant to happen. At this point Minnow was supposed to be going through the introductions: Elli, this is Kate, this is Doug, Ben's at the bar, but he'll be back in a minute. That was the plan. It was all organised. Instead . . .

Doug was centre stage, watching Jacinta, who looked like she wanted to vomit on him. Kate was sitting in a chair, mouth shocked open, watching the whole Jacinta/Doug thing, and Elli was standing beside Minnow, wearing the same expression Little Red Riding Hood must have worn when she realised that it wasn't really her grandma lying there.

Jacinta turned on Minnow, and Minnow flinched.

'You're the guy I met, aren't you?' she said. 'At Marco's? You're the guy I went home with that night. Aren't you?'

Minnow frantically searched for the explanation that was

going to work best. Something that was going to make him a hero in Elli's eyes. He looked at Jacinta. Her eyes were an icy blue, her mouth was crumbling in on itself. She looked like she was really hurting. He looked down at the floor.

'Yes,' he said.

'You're Minnow, aren't you?' she accused.

'Yes.'

She turned back to Doug and slapped him hard across the face.

'So who the fuck are you, you fucking fuck-head?' she asked.

Yep, things were going well so far.

'Jacinta,' Doug put his palms up. 'I wanted to tell you,' he said. 'I just didn't know how.'

'Tell me what? What did you want to tell me?' Jacinta frowned and shook her head, her words starting to speed up and gather momentum, like a car veering out of control towards a brick wall. 'I don't even know what's going on here. Who the fuck are you? I cannot believe that we've been together for six weeks and I don't even know your name. You make me sick. I feel like, I don't even know what I feel like. Who are you? Are you Doug?'

'Yes.'

Jacinta slapped him again.

She turned to walk out. Doug grabbed her arm. She yanked her arm away from him.

'Don't you touch me. Don't you fucking touch me. You are never to touch me again. I hope you enjoyed it last time, because that's all you've got now. The memories, you fucking arsehole.'

She sure did swear a lot.

(Just quietly, Minnow had to hand it to Doug. He'd

thought the take-Jacinta-out-and-pretend-you're-me-deal was inspired. But that Doug had kept seeing her, and kept using Minnow's name, now that was truly brilliant. Fucking fantastic.)

Doug rubbed his hand over his mouth, as if trying to erase everything he was about to say before he said it.

'I just didn't know how to tell you,' he said. 'And the longer I took, the harder it was. I should have told you the first night, but I couldn't.'

Jacinta turned on him.

'You keep saying that. "I didn't know how to tell you." I still don't know what you were going to say. You act like I know what you're talking about, but mate, I've gotta tell you, I've got no idea where you're coming from, what you wanted to say to me. And you know what? I'm not interested in any of it. I don't care what you wanted to say. I've heard enough already. You think I want to hear more?'

She turned her back on Doug. She would have stormed out, if it wasn't for all the people. She turned back to Doug.

'You took me out as a joke?'

'No,' he said, 'not as a joke. It wasn't a joke. It was just,' Doug rubbed his forehead, 'it was just, I don't know. It was just stupid.'

Jacinta looked over at Doug with a metal face. Doug looked back at her.

'I really like you, Jacinta,' he said. 'That's why I couldn't tell you the truth.'

Jacinta opened her mouth, shook her head, then closed her mouth again. Her eyes dammed up with tears. One more drop and they'd spill over her bottom lashes.

Minnow looked at Elli. Elli was standing with her arms crossed in front of her. Minnow saw Kate stand and walk in the direction of the bar. That was a good thing. Scare up those beers that Ben had gone to get. Minnow sure could do with a drink. Jacinta looked away from Doug towards the door, tilting her head to tip her tears back down her throat. Maybe tonight wasn't the best time to tell Elli he didn't really have a kid after all.

Chapter 20

Ben really liked crowds. There was something comforting about them. Enclosing. Like a gigantic hug. Each crowded room had its own unique dynamic. It was like all these people's energy, zinging off the walls, ricocheting through each other's drinks, intoxicating even the people who weren't on the booze.

And crowds were always smoky. Ben had noticed that. Encouraging you to light up. To drag that fag out of your pocket and kiss it into your mouth. Ben pulled his fags out and fired one up. The girl next to him asked for a light. She smiled at him. He smiled back. She leaned over towards him, put her hand on his arm, and said into his ear: 'No wonder they call it Crush.' Ben nodded, and had a drag of his cigarette.

He turned his attention back towards the bar, not wanting to miss an opportunity with the barmaid. He could feel the girl beside him looking over at him again. He could feel her eyes on him. She touched his arm again and said: 'It's so nice to see someone smoke. You know, everyone's so down on smokers these days. It's a major drag.'

He looked over at her and smiled. Not a smile-smile. Not the sort of smile he reserved for Kate, or any of his mates. Just a we're-standing-here-at-the-bar-together-type smile. She asked him, 'Are you here with anyone?'

'Yeah, I'm here with my girlfriend and a few friends. How about you?'

'Just some friends,' she said. 'No one special.'

Ben smiled and turned his attention back to the bar. He had a toke of his durry and tapped the ash onto the floor. That was the other thing about crowds. Crowds ashed on the floor. Gatherings didn't. Tête-à-tête's didn't. A few-friends-around didn't. But crowds did.

Ben felt someone dig their knees into the backs of his legs, making him buckle. As he turned, a voice whispered in his ear, 'Do I make you go weak at the knees?'

He smiled and put his arm around Kate's waist. 'Absolutely.'

'God,' she said. 'It's taking forever. Have you been up here the whole time?'

'No, I ran into Marco and was having a chat with him. But I suppose I've been up at the bar for about 10 minutes.'

Kate shook her head.

'How's it going over there?' Ben asked. 'Has Minnow's chick turned up yet?'

'Yep, she's here.'

'What's she like?'

'Well, let me tell you.'

Ben smiled.

'She turned up with a friend of hers. Jacinta.'

'Right.'

'You remember a couple of months ago, when Doug took

206

out that girl Jacinta, who Minnow had slept with. Remember?
And pretended to be him?'

'Yeah.'

'Well, she must be mates with Elli, because she's turned
up tonight, and now she's fully spitting it; she's calling Doug
Minnow, and Elli's calling Minnow Minnow, and they both
want to know what's going on, so I thought I'd escape and
join you here at the bar.'

Ben butted out his fag and put his arm around Kate again.

For the splittest of a split second, when Kate had said 'she
turned up with a friend of hers', he had been expecting her
to say 'Daphne' or 'Amy'. Even though he knew Minnow's
Elli wasn't his old Elli, he still half-expected them to be the
same girl. It wasn't a common name. And his Elli was a waitress too, like Minnow's. Except his Elli worked at Franco's,
not The Tea House. And his Elli didn't have a kid. Although,
he hadn't spoken to her for ages. She may have changed jobs.
She might not be at Franco's anymore. But she definitely
didn't have a kid.

'Doug's been seeing her a bit,' Kate said.

'Who?'

'Jacinta. That girl.'

'Has he?'

'Yeah. As Minnow.'

Ben laughed and shook his head.

'Those guys are unbelievable. I mean, they're good blokes,
but they're fucking shockers when it comes to girls.'

'I know.'

'I sometimes wonder — oh hang on, three Boags, and
three glasses of . . . should I get the other two girls a drink?'
Kate nodded. Definitely. 'Three vodka and tonics.'

Ben turned back towards Kate.

'I sometimes wonder how you've stayed friends with them. You're such a take-no-shit-type person, and they're so full of it.'

Kate smiled.

'I know,' she said, 'but it doesn't worry me with them. Sometimes when I tell people things they've done, I know they sound horrible. But they're always good value. Entertaining. And they were absolutely fantastic to me when I was pregnant, and after Elliot left. Plus they've always been unreal with Lochie. When I decided to study photography, Lochie was only about 18 months old, and Elliot was being a complete fuckwit about looking after him. So Minnow and Doug took care of him while I went to class. Two years worth of babysitting. And they never once asked for anything in return. They just did it. Happy to come over and look after him, play games with him. I mean, they may be complete bastards to the girls they go out with, but they've always been fantastic friends to me.'

'Yeah, that's true.'

The barmaid brought the drinks over to Ben and Kate.

'Do you need a tray?' she asked.

'No, we're right,' Ben said.

He paid, and then he and Kate picked up three glasses each and started fighting their way through the crowd. Back to Minnow and Doug.

And Elli.

Elli didn't get it.

Doug must have been seeing Jacinta on the sly behind Kate's back, so now Jacinta had left Crush, and Doug had followed after her. Elli thought he should have been trying to find Kate, instead of going after Jacinta. As soon as Kate had realised what was going on with Doug and Jacinta, she'd left the table, and Elli wouldn't mind betting that she was pretty pissed off about the whole deal.

'What about Kate?' Elli said to Minnow, as she watched Doug trying to prevent Jacinta from leaving Crush.

'What about her?' Minnow asked.

'Well, I assume that was her sitting there when we came up.'

'Yeah.'

'Well, shouldn't Doug be trying to sort things out with her?'

Minnow frowned.

'Why?'

'Well, isn't she going to be pissed off that he's been seeing Jacinta behind her back?'

Minnow laughed.

'Oh. No. He and Kate are just friends. Kate goes out with . . .'

'Kate goes out with Ben,' said a voice at Elli's back.

Elli looked up. Shit. Ben.

Elli was to have a recurring nightmare for months to come. Except it happened during the day. When she was awake. A daymare. She would be doing something totally unrelated to complete and utter personal humiliation, when suddenly she'd be overcome with this tightening in her stomach, she'd have difficulty breathing, and she'd see herself turning, turning to face — no it was too ghastly — turning to face Ben, her old Ben. And he would be grinning down at her, and she wouldn't hear him, but she'd see his mouth say 'sprung'.

And she'd look from Ben to Kate, very slowly, and see Kate frowning at Ben.

Then suddenly Kate's eyes would bloom widely and she'd look from Ben to Elli, and Elli could see Kate mouthing the words 'She's your Elli?' And she'd see Kate's mouth open in a gigantic laugh and, God no, please no more, Elli would turn in extreme slow motion to see Minnow looking up at Kate, and she could see him saying, 'What do you mean, his Elli?' and then she'd look down at her arm and see Minnow grabbing hold of it, and she'd look back up into his face and he'd be saying, 'Elli? You're his old Elli?' and she'd have to physically shake her head to toss the nightmare away.

Chapter 21

Before she worked at The Tea House, Elli had worked at a place called Franco's in St Kilda. It was right on the beach, near the marina, and she'd worked there for years. Halfway through art school she'd started there, and when she'd finished her course, she took on more and more shifts until, without even realising it, she was a full-time waitress and really enjoying herself. She kept intending to look for a job in advertising or graphic design, but it never eventuated. She really enjoyed hospitality. And she was good at it.

Franco's was where she'd learnt to make a primo coffee. In fact, she prided herself on her coffee-making skills, her barista skills, and one of her first major purchases when she'd started working full-time was a professional (just about) espresso machine for home.

Frank — Franco, but everyone called him Frank — had been the one to show her how to make a proper coffee. He'd said to her one day, 'You've got no idea, have you?'

'Excuse me,' Elli had said, putting her fists on her hips and looking at him with disdain, 'I'm Italian. Coffee runs through my blood. I don't need you to show me how to make a great "caffè". In fact, if anything, I should run you through the correct way of doing it.'

'Yeah, yeah, sure,' Frank had said dismissively, and gone ahead with his demonstration. He clicked the coffee machine twice and two small spurts of dried coffee squirted into the little filter he held beneath the opening.

He breathed deeply.

'Smell that. You see? You see how beautiful it is. Each time you release the coffee from the machine, you must take a deep breath, as far into your diaphragm as you can go. There are two reasons for this. First, so that you are filled with the sense of what you are doing, so that you are consumed by coffee, so that you don't forget it for even a moment. The other reason is because the deep breath relaxes you — no hunched shoulders, no tight neck. Tension goes into the coffee otherwise. You know how people say they can't sleep at night if they have coffee? This is bullshit. It is not because of the coffee. This is because of the tension that was brewed into the coffee by whoever made it. So.'

He pressed the coffee against a flat disc, to pack it densely.

'You know how you crush lavender to release the aroma? This is what I'm doing here. Every step, every procedure, there is a reason for it. Don't think of it as making a coffee, think of it as designing a masterpiece. Coffee is not pedestrian. It should not be treated as if it were.'

He 'up-and-clicked' the packed coffee filter into position. Two coffee cups were placed to catch each precious drop. He pressed the button. Boiling hot water steeped through the coffee, then drizzled into the cups, dark, dark, dark, the colour of Elli's hair.

Frank took a carton of milk out of the fridge and held it for Elli to touch.

'It has to be as cold as this, at least.'

He poured the milk into the metal jug and started gently 'masturbating' the milk under the steamer. That's what he actually said: 'masturbate'.

'You've got to masturbate the milk, Elli.'

'Frank, you are so lucky you're gay, otherwise I'd be going you for sexual harassment.'

'I'm just telling it as it is. Making coffee, proper coffee, the Italian way, is a very sexual thing. You masturbate the milk. You treat it gently. You make it feel good. Warm. It starts to get hot. Steamy. It is like a love affair. You and the milk. You can make the milk sensuous, delicious to drink, an experience, or you can make it have no soul. This is what you have been doing,' he started to wank the milk roughly, absent-mindedly. Then he resumed the gentle 'masturbation'.

'And you see, now it starts to froth. Not a spurting froth, a rising, a taking the breath away.'

'Yeah, I can imagine what that's supposed to represent.'

He took the jug away from the steamer and picked up a spoon to hold the froth back, while the milk plunged into the cup.

'And now,' he said, 'the final union.'

'Right,' said Elli. 'This is the orgasm part or something, is it?'

Frank stopped pouring for a moment and looked at her.

'No,' he said. 'The orgasm happened when I made the coffee. The milk is not the orgasm. The coffee is the orgasm. It's all about the coffee. If the milk was the orgasm, then what would happen when you made an espresso? Eh? No, this is after the orgasm. This is lying in bed afterwards. This is the gentle caress. Here we have the afterglow.'

'Right,' Elli said. 'Well, talking of masturbating the milk,

I think you're giving it a good tug yourself at the moment, Frank.'

Frank had smiled at her.

Elli walked in the front door of the apartment. It was 9:35.

9:35 on a Friday night, and she was home.

9:35 on not-just-any-Friday night, but on the Friday night when she was meant to have met Minnow's friends, and had dinner, and gone to see his mate's band, and it was all supposed to have been great and fabulous, and she was meant to be totally in love, and she was meant to have told him she didn't really have a kid, but it had all been totally fucked up.

Daphne came out of the bathroom, half mascaraed. Gus came out of her bedroom, half dressed.

'You're home early,' said Daphne. 'What happened?'

'What are you guys doing?' asked Elli.

'We were just about to go out and grab something to eat.'

'Do you want to go down to Franco's? I really feel like one of his coffees.'

'Sure,' said Daphne. 'It didn't go that well, huh?'

Elli looked first at Gus, then at Daphne. She felt tired. Heavy. Well and truly shitful.

'Yeah, I suppose you could say that.'

Elli rang Jacinta the next morning. The Saturday morning. The Saturday morning after the Friday night before. She was extremely hungover. The only reason she was out of bed was because she'd had to go and vomit. And get a Berocca. She had dropped the tablet into a glass of water and watched it sizzle and spit while she waited for Jacinta to pick up the phone. Jacinta's answering machine went on. This time Elli left a message.

'Hi Jacinta. It's Elli here. I'm just ringing to see how you're going. Um. I'm really sorry about what . . .'

And Jacinta picked up the phone.

'Hello?'

'Oh hi. It's me. Elli.'

'How are you going?'

'Yeah, not bad. How are you feeling?'

'Actually, I feel like shit.'

'Yeah,' Elli nodded, 'I can imagine.'

There wasn't much else to say.

'Well, I suppose you must be relieved,' said Jacinta.

'What? Because you aren't seeing my Minnow?'

'Yeah.'

'No. No, in fact I felt pretty bad for you.'

'Oh. Thanks.'

'And besides, he was a prick last night after you left.'

'Oh. Are you okay?'

'Yeah.'

Quiet again. Elli and Jacinta had never really been chums. It was hard to know where to steer the conversation when it felt so heavy and awkward.

'I suppose, at least you've got your other man anyway,' said Elli. 'Are you still seeing him?'

Jacinta coughed up a little phlegm of contempt.

'Yes. Of course. I doubt you would've got your money if we'd busted up.'

What? What did Jacinta mean 'I doubt you would've got your money if we'd busted up'?

'Although,' Jacinta continued, 'I'm really over it. He was such a pig about that whole thing. He thought I was in on it. As soon as I've saved up some money, I'm out of here.'

Elli frowned.

'What do you mean?' she asked.

'He thought I knew,' said Jacinta.

'Who?'

'Steven.'

'What?'

Elli wasn't keeping up at all. It seemed quite simple, except there was a fundamental something that was missing.

'Thought you knew what?' Elli asked.

'About the letter.'

'What letter?'

'What do you mean, "what letter"?' Jacinta asked in an impatient voice. 'What letter do you think?'

Elli leaned forward into the phone. There was definitely some kind of connection problem.

'Are you talking about the letter Daphne and I sent?'

'Yes. What else would I be talking about?'

'Did your boyfriend get it?'

'Are you trying to annoy me?'

There was no need for that, Elli thought.

'Why do you think you got paid?'

Nuh. Elli still didn't get it.

'Are you saying we got paid because I know you?'

'What?'

Now Jacinta sounded really irritable, and Elli felt that wasn't really called for. She just didn't get what Jacinta was talking about.

'Did he pay us because I work with you?'

'Well, duh. Actually, while we're on the subject, how did you find out about us anyway?'

'That you were seeing each other?'

'Yeah.'

'Because you said you were.'

'I may have said I was seeing someone. I never told you his name.'

'No.'

'So how did you find out it was Steven?'

'I didn't.'

'What?'

'I didn't. I still don't know. What's his surname?'

'Elli,' Jacinta said.

'I don't. He sent a note with the money, but he didn't write his surname. We've been busting to know who he was.'

'Well, hang on a sec. He got a letter from you addressed to him. What do you mean you don't know who he is? Obviously you know who he is.'

'No, we sent that letter to everyone on the Richest 100 list. Your Steven wasn't the only guy to get it.'

'Omigod,' said Jacinta.

'What? There were 17 Stevens. We counted. That's why I still don't know who you're going out with, because there were so many of them on our list.'

'Omigod,' Jacinta said again, and burst out laughing. 'Omigod. So it wasn't a blackmail letter.'

'Blackmail. Shit no. Omigod.'

And then they'd both burst out laughing.

'Steven Rickards. That's who sent you the money,' said Jacinta. 'I can't believe you didn't know. He gave me so much shit about it.'

'You're having an affair with Steven Rickards? Shit.'

'Well, sort of. I mean, I am, but I don't want to anymore. I'm moving out as soon as I've got some funds saved.'

'And he thought you were in on the blackmailing thing?'

'Yep.'

'Shit.'

There was a bit of silence. Elli was grinning widely. Steven Rickards thought they'd been blackmailing him. Cool.

'You should move in here,' Elli said. 'Daphne's looking for someone to share with while I'm away.'

'Is she? Wouldn't that be funny. Steven would definitely think I was in on it if I moved into your place. I don't think I will, thanks for the offer though.'

'Fair enough. So what are you going to do about Doug, then?'

Jacinta sighed.

'You know, I don't know. I think what he did is so low, I don't think I could ever forgive him. I don't think I could go out with him, knowing that it had all been a setup. That that's the type of guy he is. I just don't know if I could ever trust him. You know?'

'Yeah, I know what you mean.'

Elli had a slug of her Berocca.

She saw Ben standing there, mouthing the word 'sprung'. She saw Kate looking from Ben to Elli and laughing. She felt Minnow grab her arm. It was all so awful, she couldn't bear to think about it. It was so humiliating. So embarrassing. So awfully awful.

Horrible.

She had looked at Ben and thought maybe he might keep quiet about her not having a kid. And then she had looked at Kate and knew there wasn't a chance.

'Anyway, I've gotta go and do a few things,' said Jacinta. 'Thanks for calling, I appreciate it. I'll see you at work.'

'Yeah, okay.'

Elli sat on the couch, the phone on her lap. She had another sip of her drink. When Minnow had grabbed her arm, a gush of frantic thoughts had swept over her. She wanted to leave. She wanted to go to the toilet. She wanted to leave the table and go to the toilet, then Ben could tell Minnow and when she came back, at least Minnow would know. At least she wouldn't have to tell him. At least she wouldn't have to look into his eyes and tell him she'd lied. But looking at his face, she realised he knew already. He knew, as soon as he'd said, 'Ben's old Elli', that she didn't have a kid. And she wished she could sit and tell him, just the two of them, explain that it was an awful mistake, that she hadn't meant it to continue, but it had been too hard.

It had been like watching a full glass of wine tip onto the table. You saw it happening, you were that close, but you couldn't do a thing to stop it. Minnow had frowned at her. She'd watched him, his expression tipping into anger, just like that, that's how close she was, and she couldn't do a thing to stop it. Minnow had stood up and walked out. Left. Gone.

Ben had sat down with her. Kate had left to find Minnow. Of all the things in all the world, when you catch up with your ex and his new girlfriend, you want to look like you're the one woman he should never have left. You're a force, a triumph, desirable, attractive, together. Life is good. He should never have let you slip through his fingers. He should never have let you go. You're an enigma. The one he wonders about forever. The what-if girl of his past.

So Elli sat snivelling beside Ben, snivelling, his arm around her, comforting her, telling her that Minnow didn't really have a kid either, and it was all even more horrible than she could have ever imagined. She went to the Ladies and blew her nose on some toilet paper. She didn't even know what she was crying about. She wasn't sad, she was angry. Pissed off. Furious. But she couldn't stop crying. It was ridiculous. She splashed water on her face and looked at herself in the mirror. Her hair was wet around her face, her mascara was now half-strength at best, her lips looked a dull, matte bit-redder-than-normal colour.

And then, just when things couldn't get much worse, Mona walked into the bathroom. You know, Mona — that chick from Minnow's work. The receptionist. She'd looked at Elli.

'Are you okay?' she'd asked.

Yeah, sure. Fine. Perfectly okay. No problems here.

'You're so lucky,' Elli said. 'He's a complete arsehole. He doesn't even have a kid. Did you know that? He made it up. It's all crap. It's a lie. It's not true. And then he goes and makes me feel like shit, but he's worse.'

'What do you mean, he doesn't have a kid?'

'What do you think I mean?' asked Elli, rubbing her eyes, rubbing mascara all over her cheek. 'He's a bullshitter. He's a fucking liar. He doesn't have a kid. He treats women like shit. He wouldn't even stay to talk about it. He roots around. He's awful. I don't know what I saw in him. I'm glad I don't have to work with a cunt like that.'

Extreme times call for extreme words. Mona's mouth looked like it was wrapping itself around a smile. Elli slammed out of the bathroom. Minnow had left her because he found out she didn't really have a kid, and now Ben had told her that Minnow didn't really have one either. If they weren't both so fucked up, she'd almost think they were perfect for each other.

Ben had walked her to her car. There was no sign of Kate and Minnow anywhere.

'Sorry I can't stay with you,' he'd said, 'but I've gotta go to The Espy and set up.'

'Don't worry about it. I'm fine.'

Sure she was. She looked up at Ben. He was nice. And handsome. And it was good because she looked at him and genuinely couldn't imagine what she'd seen in him in the first place. Like, he played in a groovy band, and he was cool and all that, but he was maybe a bit too serious. Serious about his music. Serious about his girlfriend. Serious about things.

That's what she liked about Minnow. That he was so not-serious. He was always mucking around. Cracking jokes. Even though that thing with Jacinta and Doug had been really awful, she could imagine him coming up with the idea, thinking it would be really funny. He would have figured Jacinta would never find out, and what she didn't know wouldn't hurt her. In a way, she hadn't even been surprised when Ben had told her Minnow didn't really have a kid. Like, she'd been totally spun-out, but at the same time, it didn't really surprise her.

It was typical of him.

She sat on the couch, the phone limp in her lap, the empty Berocca glass on the coffee table. She looked up and saw Daphne standing in the doorway.

'Hi,' Daphne said.

'Hi back,' said Elli.

Daphne came and sat down beside her.

'How are you feeling?'

'Bad.'

'Have you spoken to him?' Daphne asked, looking at the phone.

'No,' she said. 'I just called Jacinta to see how she was going. But guess what?' and she told Daphne what Jacinta had just told her.

'Omigod,' said Daphne. 'Steven Rickards thought we were blackmailing him? How hysterical. But how could he have? There wasn't one thing threatening in the whole letter.'

'Guilty conscience, I suppose,' said Elli, a smile blossoming on her mouth. She stretched her arms and rubbed her face, pushing her hair out of her eyes.

'Are you going to call Minnow?' Daphne asked.

'Are you kidding? There is no way. In fact, if he rings, I don't want to speak to him. You can answer it, and tell him to get fucked from me. I still can't believe that he left last night. What a fuckwit.'

'Yeah. That's bad. Well, you always said he wasn't really right for you anyway, right from the start. So it looks like you were on the money.'

'Yeah. That's vaguely satisfying, I suppose.'

But it didn't feel satisfying at all.

'I feel so hungover,' said Daphne.

'Same.'

'I don't think I needed those Sambucas.'

'No. Me either.'

'Do you know, the only time I ever have a Sambuca is when I'm totally trashed. I don't know why I do it. It's like,

I never feel like a Sambuca, but when I'm drunk, I really get a taste for it. Have you had a Berocca?'

'Yeah.'

'I think I need one of those too.'

Daphne got off the couch and walked towards the kitchen.

'I might get one for Gus as well.'

Elli watched as Daphne walked back to her bedroom carrying two plum-red drinks, fizzing wildly. She looked down at the phone. It was silent. She wondered what she'd do if it rang now, while Daphne was in bed. She'd probably let the answering machine get it. Fuck him.

She went to have a shower. It might make her feel a smidge better. And it did — until she felt nauseous and had to go vomit again. Then she felt a lot worse. She went back to bed and lay there for a while, vaguely dozing, waking up, feeling sick, wishing she could sleep through it, going back to sleep, waking up. Feeling awful.

She got up again about one. Daphne was sitting on the couch, doing the cryptic crossword.

'Where's Gus?'

'He's gone to play tennis with Hugh and some friends of theirs. How are you feeling?'

'Terrible. Has Minnow called?'

'No.'

'Bastard.'

She sat on the couch, waiting for the phone to ring so Daphne could say Elli wasn't speaking. But he didn't call, so Elli had to ring him herself.

'Hello?' he said.

'I'm not ringing to speak to you. I don't want to have a conversation with you. I'm just ringing to tell you I think you're a complete fuckwit, and I never want to see you again, and I certainly don't want you coming overseas with me. I couldn't think of anything worse.'

'Did you want to speak to Minnow?'

'Oh. Sorry. Who's this?'

'No, it's me. I was just kidding.'

She hung up on him. He rang back, and Daphne told him Elli didn't want to speak to him. About three, he came around. Daphne answered the door. Elli was sitting watching telly and could hear them in the doorway. Daphne came into the lounge room.

'Do you want to see him?'

'No.'

'Okay.'

'No, actually, I do want to see him.'

'Okay.'

'Do you think I should?'

'I don't know. It's your call.'

'Okay. I'll see him.'

Daphne went and brought him into the lounge room. Then she left the two of them alone. Minnow looked at Elli and grinned.

'So, you don't really have a kid?'

Elli frowned at him.

'Why did you walk out last night?' she asked.

'I don't know. It was, I don't know. I'm not sure.'

Daphne came back into the lounge room. She looked at Elli, ignored Minnow.

'I'm going round to Gus's. Do you want to come?'

'No. I'm right. I'll see you later.'

Daphne gave Elli an encouraging smile, then left. Minnow sat there. Elli sat there. Neither spoke. Finally, he said, 'Nice place,' or something pathetic like that, and she just looked at him like he was a fish milkshake.

'I don't know why you came around,' she said. 'You obviously didn't come here to apologise, or tell me what was going on last night, or anything like that, so I think it's best you go. I mean, if you wanted to talk, that'd be great, but if you just want to sit here and assess my interior decoration, then piss off. I'm not interested.'

Minnow stood up. Elli stayed on the couch, looking at her fingernails. And then, she's still not sure quite how it happened, but they were in her bedroom with all their clothes off, and he was on top of her. He felt warm and strong and his arms were flexed, holding her tight, and his tongue was in her mouth, and all over her body at the same time, and it was exactly as it was meant to be. He was kissing her and she was kissing him, and it didn't really matter that he didn't have a kid, because she didn't have one either. It was almost synergy.

Or something like that.

Postscript

Warren Bourke, Human Resources Manager of Radio 625 FM, looked up from his desk. Mona was standing in his doorway. He smiled at her.

'Hi Mona. Is everything okay?'

'Yeah.'

She didn't say anything further. Just stood there.

'Did you want to talk to me?' he asked.

Mona started fiddling with her necklace.

'Yeah, actually, I did.'

'Well, come on in. Sit down.'

Mona came on in. She sat down. She looked slyly at him across his desk, before looking down at her lap. Warren smiled. He raised his eyebrows.

'How can I help you, Mona?' he asked.

'Well, you see, Warren,' Mona said, looking up at him, 'I heard something on the weekend, and I thought it might interest you.'

'Right. Great. Well,' he cocked his finger like a friendly pistol at her. He pulled the trigger. 'Shoot.'

She smiled.

'You see,' she looked back down at her lap, before looking up again to make sure Warren was paying close attention, 'it's about Minnow.' She leaned forward, towards Warren. 'And his kid.'

She leaned back in her chair. Warren was listening.

Pow.

Acknowledgments

Waiter, a glass of your finest champagne for these people:

Olga Lorenzo, a fantastic teacher who laughed at all my jokes and encouraged me to send my first chapter in as a short story to *HQ* magazine, which led me to meeting Linda, which led me to being published.

Linda Funnell, my publisher who took a punt on an unfinished manuscript by an unpublished author. I hope I don't let you down.

Kate Pollard, my editor, who made the entire editing process fun, easy and not even a bit stressful. By the way Kate, I hope you find those elusive 'perfect shoes' you're after.

Belinda Lee, my senior editor, who tag-teamed with Kate, to help fix up my shoddy structure, appalling mistakes in continuity and terrible spelling.

Katie Mitchell for a great cover design and page layout, Mel Cain for some fabbo PR-ing, and all the other people at HarperCollins who helped get this book onto shelves (and then hopefully off shelves and onto bedside tables).

Tim Brierley, a fantastic friend and a spot-on critic who didn't pull any punches (actually, while we're on the subject of pulling punches, you might like to be a bit more gentle with me, next book).

Samantha Castle, my great work buddy, who read the first few chapters and was unstintingly positive about everything I wrote.

Hendo, for being incredibly encouraging and positive and inspiring and enthusiastic.

Lindy, for not liking the first chapter, but looking forward to reading the rest of the book anyway. A true friend.

Simonette and Andrew for big laughs, small cards and bunches of flowers.

My fabulous friends: Sally, for helping me keep my blood sugar levels up. Liz, for an essential part of the story (you'll know it when you see it). Alison, for a delicious bottle of Veuve. Gin, for her unexpected connections. Peter Bof for ideas and input during the last stages. David and Janine for their gorgeous card. Anne Connors for bolstering my confidence at every opportunity. Bardo, Thommo, Ringo, Robbo and Wilbur for 'nahbeda'.

Peter, a fantastic brother and babysitter, who helped me nail down aspects of certain male characters by forwarding me some particularly chauvinistic e-mails. By the way, he's single, if anyone's interested.

Dominique and Harry, my two gorgeous angels, for not pestering me when I was writing. Well, not much. Well, especially not after I'd yelled at them.

Charlie, our gorgeous baby, for sleeping to my strict writing schedule.

And finally, Andrew, the most totally fantastic husband a girl could possibly ever ask for. Waiter, a whole bottle for this bloke. Thank you for holding my hand all the way through this — it made it difficult while I was typing, but I always knew I could rely on you to be totally honest and prevent me from mailing any humour disasters to Kate, my editor. A girl could never be a commitment-phobe with a guy like you around.